WHISPER

night roamers
book one

KRISTEN MIDDLETON

Copyright ©2020 by Kristen Middleton

All rights reserved. All rights reserved under the International and Pan-American Copyright Conventions. No part of this book may be reproduced or transmitted in any form or by any means, electronic or mechanical, including photocopying, recording, or by any information storage and retrieval system, without permission in writing from the publisher. The author acknowledges the trademark owners of various products referenced in this work of fiction, which has been used without permission. The publication/use of these trademarks is not authorized, associated with, or sponsored by the trademark owners.

This is a work of fiction. Names, places, characters and incidents are either the product of the author's imagination or are used fictitiously, and any resemblance to any actual persons, living or dead, organizations, events or locales is entirely coincidental.

Warning: the unauthorized reproduction or distribution of this copyrighted work is illegal. Criminal copyright infringement, including infringement without monetary gain, is investigated by the FBI and is punishable by up to 5 years in prison and a fine of $250,000.

PROLOGUE

EMINEM'S LATEST SONG blasted through the speakers at Gil Fisher's graduation party. It was the largest kegger she'd ever attended and everyone was having a blast. She been enjoying herself too... until stepping into the garage and finding Bailey Carter and Lacy Vanderhoven, making out by the keg. Seeing them together felt like someone had hit her in the stomach with a sledgehammer.
Asshole.
Bailey had been the main reason she'd even gone to the party. He'd personally invited her and she'd been crushing on him since the tenth grade. With his messy, sun-bleached hair, light green eyes, and gorgeous smile, he was the epitome of hotness. Now, Tina felt stupid for even thinking she had a chance with someone like him. Especially seeing Prom Queen Lacy in his arms.
Screw them.
College was only three months away and she'd be free of Shore Lake and all the idiot guys she'd gone to high school with.
Trying not to cry, Tina turned around and went in search of Amy, her best friend. She found her outside, by the bonfire.
"Did you find Bailey?" Amy asked.
Tina told her what she'd seen.
"What a dickhead."

"Yeah, well, it's no big deal. They can have each other."

"Exactly."

Tina remembered the joint in her purse. Now was as good of a time as any. Especially after what had just happened. "You wanna get high?"

Amy slapped at a mosquito. "No. I'm already feeling pretty buzzed as it is."

"Not even one hit?"

"The last time I tried smoking pot, I threw up." She looked around. "Anyway, I feel like this party is going to be busted soon. It's getting too crazy."

As if to prove her point, someone lit off a bottle rocket. It exploded high above them and people started cheering.

"Yeah, you're probably right."

Amy sighed. "Maybe we should leave?"

Tina didn't want to, however. She'd told her parents that she was sleeping over at Amy's, which was a lie. So she had the entire night to do whatever she wanted.

"In a little while. I wanna spark up the joint first." Tina dug into her purse and pulled it out. "You sure you don't want a couple hits?"

"No. Seriously, I'm good."

"Okay." Not wanting to share with anyone else, she told Amy she was going down by the lake. "You want to at least keep me company?"

Before Amy could reply, Bryce Freeman walked over and put his arm around her shoulders. "Hey, beautiful. I brought that strawberry schnapps you were asking about. You want some?"

Amy's eyes lit up and she smiled. "Yeah."

Tina gave her a dirty look. "Though you were worried about driving?"

Bryce snorted. "Chill out, *Mom*. She doesn't have to drink the entire bottle. One shot won't hurt her."

"I'll just have a little," Amy added.
Tina hated Bryce. He was bossy, manipulative, and conceited. His parents had money and he was always bragging about it. Amy thought he was hot, however, and would do almost anything for the guy. He had a girlfriend, however. That never stopped him from flirting with everyone in sight.
"You want any?" Bryce asked Tina.
Normally she would, but being around him annoyed her. "No."
"Suit yourself. We'll be up in the kitchen. That's where the hard stuff is." He started maneuvering Amy toward the house.
Amy looked back at her over her shoulder. "I'll come find you when we're done. Okay?"
Tina sighed. "Fine."
She mouthed the word "Sorry."
Tina shrugged.
They disappeared inside and Tina headed toward the woods. A few minutes later, she was leaning against a tree and staring at the calm lake, still trying to forget about Bailey and Lacy. She took a puff of the joint and held it in for a few seconds before releasing the sweet, pungent smoke. Already feeling calmer, she sighed in contentment and closed her eyes.
"Hey."
Startled, Tina turned around and saw a familiar face. One that also made her nervous.
"You scared the shit out of me. You shouldn't sneak up on people like that."
He smiled. "Sorry. What are you doing?"
Tina held up the joint. "Just chillin' out. Relaxing."
He stared at her curiously. "And that helps?"
"For me it does. Haven't you ever gotten high?"
"No."
"You want to try a hit?"

He stopped next to her. "Sure, why not?"

She handed him the joint and told him what to do. He inhaled and held it in. Unlike most newbies, he exhaled but didn't cough.

"Wow, you're a natural," she replied before taking another hit herself.

"Thanks."

"You feel anything yet? This is some strong shit."

Looking amused, he shook his head. "Nope."

"Want any more?"

"Nah."

Feeling anxious about being alone with him, she put the joint out. "So, what are you doing here?"

"I came to see you."

"Me? Why?"

His eyes began to glow an eerie red. "I think you already know."

Her heart leaped into her throat. In the back of her mind, she had an idea of what he was talking about. There'd been rumors. Crazy, wild ones about him and his friends. She'd laughed them off, but seeing his eyes glow was some freaky shit.

Trying not to panic, she forced a smile to her face. "It's getting late. I have to go back to the party."

His lip twitched. "It doesn't have to be like this."

Her pulse drummed in her ears. *I have to get out of here.*

"I can make it good for you," he added.

Terrified, Tina dropped the joint and started running up the hill, back to the safety of the party. Right before she reached the top, his hand landed firmly on her shoulder. He twisted her around and pinned her gaze with his.

Tears flooded her eyes. "Please don't hurt me," she squeaked.

He trailed his finger down her cheek and smiled. "Soon, you'll be begging me to."
Tina didn't understand what he meant.
Not until later…

1

"MOM LEFT THE door unlocked," I hollered at my twin brother, Nathan.

He slammed the door to his '67 Mustang. "That's weird." He brushed a hand through his sandy-brown hair and shoved his keys into his jean pocket. "You know how she's always nagging us about it."

"I know, right?" I held the front door open for him. "I guess the rules only apply to us."

"Apparently."

Mom was married to a cop once. Our father. He'd drilled it into all our heads about locking the door, even when we were home. Now that they were divorced, she'd been especially adamant about keeping everything secure and had even talked about getting a dog.

Nathan followed me into the kitchen and opened the refrigerator. He sighed and scratched his chin. "There's never anything good to eat in this place."

I set my backpack down on the floor. "Seriously? How can you still be hungry after eating that monster burger and malt?"

We'd just returned from Grannie's Malt Shop, where we'd pigged out on burgers and shakes with some friends. It was the last day of school and we were officially seniors. No more schoolwork, tests, or girls grilling me about Nathan. The guy was a major flirt and being his messenger was annoying as hell.

He flexed his bicep. "I'm going to the gym later and these guns need ammo."

I snorted a laugh and shook my head.

Nathan began rummaging through the refrigerator and pulled out the milk carton. "Just 'cause you're a string-bean doesn't mean everyone else has to eat like a bird."

I pulled out my cell phone and started checking my messages. "If I eat like a bird, it's the large yellow one from Sesame Street. I devoured almost as much as you did."

"That's right you did, Big Bird." He raised the milk carton to his lips and was about to take a swig, when we both heard a faint noise.

Stiffening up, I turned to Nathan. "What in the hell was that?"

His eyebrows knitted together. "It sounds like—"

That was when we both heard it again. Someone was sobbing.

My stomach dropped. "It sounds like Mom. Isn't she supposed to be at work?"

"Yeah." He slammed down the milk and rushed out of the kitchen.

I chased after him up the stairs and we stopped outside of her bedroom door. The sounds were definitely coming from her room.

Nathan knocked on the door. "Mom?"

She moaned.

He looked at me. "What do I do?"

"Go in," I urged.

Nathan opened the door and peeked his head inside. "Oh, my God."

I pushed him forward and that was when I saw her lying naked on the floor next to the bed. Her face was swollen and bleeding. Her body was badly bruised.

Both of us stood frozen in shock for a second before rushing to her side. I kneeled down next to her while Nathan covered her with a blanket from her bed. She looked like she was in so much pain; I was afraid to even touch her. "Mom?"

She opened one of her black-rimmed eyes. "Call the police," she whimpered, barely coherent.

I grabbed the phone and dialed nine-one-one. I couldn't remember much of the conversation, only that the operator promised to send help while trying to console me.

"Is the assailant still in the house?" the woman asked.

I looked at Nathan. "If he was, we'd need the morgue, too." My brother was very protective of our mother. If he'd caught the asshole who did this, he'd have gone ape-shit.

The woman sighed. "Tell everyone to remain calm. Lock the door and wait for the ambulance. They should be arriving shortly."

"Thank you." I ended the call and turned around. "They're sending help."

Mom nodded. "Good."

I felt so helpless and frightened for her. We had no idea of the injuries she'd sustained. She could be bleeding internally for all we knew.

Nathan, who was kneeling next to her, brushed the hair out of her eyes gently. "Mom, what happened?"

She didn't answer, but to me, it was pretty obvious. The woman had been attacked and raped.

I got down on my knees next to her again. I had so many questions but wasn't sure if it was the right time to ask. She was obviously in a lot of pain. I grabbed her hand and held it. Seeing her like this broke my heart. "Can I help you with anything?"

She let out a shaky breath. "I should probably get dressed before the paramedics and police arrive. Could you find me something to wear, Nikki?"

"Of course." I stood up and went over to her dresser.

"Mom?" prodded Nathan. "Can you tell us what happened?"

She opened her mouth to reply, but couldn't seem to get the words out.

I pulled him aside. "Nathan, leave her be," I murmured. "She's been raped. She probably doesn't want to talk about it right now."

Not with her son, anyway.

He looked torn up inside. "I understand that, but we need to find out who did this. If she knows the asshole, we can send the cops after him."

He had a valid point.

I kneeled back down next to her. "Mom, do you know the person who did this to you?"

She nodded.

Nathan and I looked at each other in surprise. I think we'd both expected her to say it was some stranger.

"Who was it?" Nathan asked.

Her eyes filled with tears. "Your father."

2

"ARE WE ALMOST there?" I asked, staring through my sunglasses at the endless rows of cornfields. We'd been driving for hours through the countryside and I could no longer tell the difference from one town to the next. More than anything, I just wanted to get out of the car and stretch my stiff legs.

Mom cleared her throat. "Pretty soon."

Nathan was following us in his Mustang, and I glanced back to see him talking on his cell phone once again.

"Oh, Lord," I said, leaning my head back against the headrest. "He must be talking to Deanna for the tenth time. She just won't get over the fact that we're really moving."

Mom tightened her hands on the steering wheel and glanced at me. She looked miserable. "I'm sorry about having to uproot the two of you. Especially in your last year of school. I feel so shitty about it."

I groaned. "Mom, seriously, it's not your fault. I can't even believe you're feeling guilty about it. I mean, nobody had any idea that Dad could be so violent."

It had been less than three months since our father had brutally attacked our mother. They'd been separated for the last couple of years because of his sporadic temper tantrums, along with his inability to stop screwing other women. When she'd finally found the courage to leave him, he'd actually been pretty civil about it. That was—until he'd learned she'd moved on emotionally and had started dating again. After hearing about it from a mutual friend, he'd flown into a jealous rage, striking back at her viciously. We were all still stunned about the horrifying ordeal.

"I just wish they could locate him," she said, staring straight ahead. "I think the not knowing where he is scares me the most."

I nodded. I was so ashamed, that any thoughts of him made me physically ill. It was still really hard to believe that our own father was capable of being so violent. It made it even more disturbing that he'd been in law enforcement and responsible for keeping people safe.

"Me, too."

After the attack, Dad had disappeared. Meanwhile, our mother had spent several nights in the hospital recovering. Thankfully, there's been no internal bleeding, although she'd sustained a lot of bruising. The worst of the damage had been done to her mentally. In fact, when she was finally released from the hospital, she couldn't sleep at night without drugs. She'd wake up in the middle of the night, terrified that he'd show up and beat her again. Then, just recently, she'd been given a gift—a way out. Her employer had offered her an accounting job in Montana, and that was where the three of us were now headed to start a new life.

"I think it's good that Nathan's getting away from Deanna, anyway. She's so whiny and annoying."

Mom smiled wryly. "Now, Nikki, you haven't liked any of Nathan's girlfriends."

"It's not my fault he attracts the psychos."

She burst out laughing and I smiled, enjoying a sound that was finally finding its way back into our lives again.

"God, you're awful," she said, shaking her head in amusement.

"Oh, come on. You know I'm right."

She grabbed her Ray-Bans from the center column and put them on. "Well, he is a little too young to be tied down to just one girl. So, if you ask me, this move will be healthy for the both of them."

"I'm sure Deanna will find someone else by next week, anyway." She was so damn needy. Watching her cling to Nathan all the time had been nauseating.

"You really don't like her, do you?"

I shrugged.

Deep down, I knew I wasn't being totally fair, because the truth was, I was a little jealous. My brother and I had always been very close, especially living in such a dysfunctional family environment. My earliest memories were of my parents constantly arguing and accusing each other of things. They'd yelled and fought so much of our lives, that once he'd left, the quietness had been eerie. And through it all we'd weathered the storms together. In fact, for all our lives, we'd been best friends; sharing and doing everything together. That was, until the tenth grade, when he'd discovered boobs, I mean, girls. Of course I'd discovered boys as well. I'd discovered that most of them in my school were crude, boring, or just plain idiots.

"So, Mom," I said, changing a subject in which, I had to admit, left me feeling a little guilty. "What were you saying about this place we're renting?"

She grinned. "I guess it's just breathtaking. It's a log cabin on Shore Lake that's been on the market for some time. The owners are related to Ernie, and because of our circumstances, they're letting us rent it relatively cheap."

Ernie was my mom's boss, a really nice old man. He was almost like a father-figure to her, which was good

because both of her parents had passed away several years ago. Aside from us, there really was nobody else.
"The cabin does sound really cool. Do they happen to have a boat or jet-skis?"
"I'm not sure about the jet-skis, but they definitely have a boat."
"Sweet."
"Ernie says he's caught *hundreds* of walleye on the lake, so we'll have to do some fishing, too."
"Yeah, I wouldn't mind that either."
"What's wrong?"
I pulled down the visor. "I have something in my eye."
"Oh."
After removing an eyelash out, I examined my reflection in the mirror. Sandy brown hair, light blue eyes, and decent cheekbones. Pretty average-looking and nothing spectacular. My mother claimed that I looked exactly like her when she was growing up. Most of Nathan's friends said she was a hot MILF, which *was* pretty gross, but I guessed that meant there was still hope for me.
I closed the visor and leaned my head back against the seat. "I wonder what the school is going to be like."
As an introvert, I was definitely feeling some anxiety about it. Unlike Nathan, the chatterbox and social butterfly.
"Ernie didn't say much, but honestly, I don't expect him to know. He's in his seventies and never had children."
"Oh, well. I'm sure it will be fine."
I didn't want her worrying about me. She was the one who needed the extra support from us, and I wasn't about to make her feel any more guilty about moving than she already did.

She slapped her fingers on the steering wheel. "Oh, I forgot to tell you, there's an extra computer at the cabin and you're allowed to use it."

"Really? That's cool," I smiled. Although she had a laptop, I'd been nagging her forever about getting a computer of my own. Not only would we need it for homework, I loved writing poems and had hoped to one day become an author. Most of mine were written in old notebooks and so hard to keep track of.

"Yes, but you'll have to share it with your brother."

"Great," I said dryly.

"I'm sure he's learned his lesson."

"I hope so."

When Nathan had been in middle school, he and some friends had borrowed her old laptop to surf the internet. Apparently, they'd "accidentally" found themselves on a porn site, and she'd gotten a virus. After dealing with that, she banned him from using her computer again.

"Are you still writing your poems?" she asked.

I nodded.

"Maybe they'll have some kind of writing club you can join in the new school?"

"Maybe."

"If not, you could always join the track team or the cheerleading squad."

I snorted. "Me? Really? When have you ever known me to be interested in cheerleading? Besides, I'm sure the girlson the squad have been doing it since elementary school. They'd laugh me right out of tryouts."

"Oh, you never know."

"It's not my thing. I'm also not into running for fun."

"What about soccer or basketball?"

I laughed. "Basketball? I think you need to be taller than the ball to play."

She chuckled. "Sorry. You got the short gene from me."

I was only five-foot-two. She was slightly taller.

"How in the hell did Nathan get the better end of the stick?" He was almost six-foot tall. "I mean, we're twins. Not that I expect him to be as short as me. It's just weird."

"Stuff like that just happens that way sometimes. Anyway, think of it this way, you have more choices in guys."

I grunted. "What is that supposed to mean?"

"Even the short ones can be tall, dark, and handsome."

"Yay," I said dryly. "I'd still rather be normal height."

"Oh, Nikki. You *are* normal height and very pretty. Once you start school, I'm sure the guys will be flocking. Just be picky about who you choose to go out with."

"Don't hold your breath."

"What do you mean?"

"High school guys like sporty, outgoing girls. Or sluts. I'm neither."

She looked amused. "Although I'm glad you're not a slut, you shouldn't be so hard on yourself. You have a lot of great qualities. Don't sell yourself short."

I wasn't even interested in meeting anyone at the moment. Most of the girls at my old school had been constantly stressed out because of their immature boyfriends. I wasn't about to go down that road, especially in my last year of high school. "It doesn't matter."

She frowned. "Sure it does. You'll want to go to all the dances, and then there's the prom. You don't want to miss out on all the fun. You'll regret it later."

"Didn't you go with dad to the prom?" I asked, then immediately felt rotten when I saw the bitterness in her eyes.

"I did," she said slowly. "But he wasn't always so... volatile. And, really, he's among the very few out there like that. You know, Nikki, you can't be afraid of the world because your dad has some issues."

Yeah, but weren't we running because she was still very much afraid?

Of course, I didn't dare mention that. Instead, I just changed the subject.

"So, how much farther of a drive do we have?" I'd noticed the mountains coming up in the distance, which had to be a good sign.

"Oh, just a couple more hours."

"Good."

She turned on the radio and tried looking for some music. It was either country or static. Frustrated, she plugged in her phone. Seconds later, Adele began to sing about *Rumors*.

I stretched my arms and yawned.

"Honey," she said, lowering her sunglasses down, "you look beat. Why don't you try and get some rest? I'll wake you when we get there."

"Okay." I closed my eyes and eventually fell asleep.

3

I WOKE UP to the sound of mom and Nathan arguing. I opened my eyes and noticed we were parked by a small grocery store.

"Why not, Mom? I just don't understand," protested Nathan, who was standing outside her door and pouting.

She sighed. "Can we *please* talk about Deanna later?"

I groaned. "Oh, God, not now." It was getting dark and we'd missed dinner and my stomach was protesting. I was cranky, and the last thing I needed was to hear any more drama about Deanna.

"Can't she just stay with us the week before school starts?" Nathan pled. "She's having a rough time with her parents, and now that I'm gone, things have gotten even worse. It's not fair for her."

Mom shook her head. "No, we have too much to do with unpacking and getting ready for school. Maybe she can come and visit sometime after it starts. Maybe at the end of September?"

"This is all bullshit," he snapped, backing up from the window. He waved his hand toward the road in exasperation. "We could have stayed home. I would've protected you. Now we're forced to move, and you didn't even give me a chance."

This was too much. Now *I* was angry. "Seriously, Nathan? You're being totally unreasonable. Mom's been through so much shit and all you care about is your stupid girlfriend. God, you're being an asshole."

He glared at me. "*I'm* being unreasonable? Why don't you just stay out of it? You don't know what it's like because you're not leaving anyone behind. You couldn't care less where we live."

He was right but it still hurt. Especially when he pointed it out that way. "I just want her safe." I folded my arms across my chest. "Apparently, you're more worried about your love life than what happens to her."

He growled in the back of his throat. "That's bullshit!"

Mom put her hand in the air. "Whoa. Okay, let's all settle down. Quit pointing fingers at each other and enough with the swearing. It doesn't help the situation."

"Sorry," I mumbled.

Nathan didn't say anything.

"Listen, it isn't either of your faults, okay? And, Nathan," she smiled sadly, "I'm grateful that you want to protect me, but you can't possibly follow me around twenty-four hours a day, nor do I expect you to be my personal bodyguard. Now, as far as Deanna goes, we'll talk about it later. *Comprende?*"

He nodded but was still sulking; I could tell this conversation was far from over.

She noticed it as well and rubbed her forehead in frustration. "Okay, let's get the things we need in the grocery store before it gets dark. I don't want to get lost while searching for this cabin."

"I agree. Let's go." I opened the door and got out of the car.

Nathan followed us into the store, still moping.

"Nathan, would you please cheer up?" Mom pleaded when we were in the frozen pizza section and he refused to pick out food.

"Yeah," I said. "Don't ruin our first night here because of a girl who's probably lining up her next soul-mate as we speak."

"Would you *shut-up*?" he snapped. "You're just jealous."

Clenching my fists, I took a step toward him. "Excuse me? Jealous?"

"Stop it!" growled Mom, getting into both of our faces. "We're in public and you're both acting... ridiculous. Now, I'm sorry that we had to move, I really am. But we're here now and there's no turning back. So get it together, or I swear to God, I won't buy any ice cream."

Nathan raised his hands in the air. "Whoa, mom, just settle down. You're right. This has gotten way out of hand. We can talk about this, no need to bring ice cream into the equation." He smirked. "That's cruel even for you."

She relaxed. "That's what I thought." She then turned to me. "What about you? Are you going to lay off Deanna, who isn't even here to defend herself?"

"Fine," I replied tightly. "As long as he stops talking about her every five minutes."

He gave me a dirty look. "Whatever."

She closed her eyes and rubbed the bridge of her nose. "You know, maybe this was a mistake, I don't know." She opened her eyes. "But, what's done is done, *and* we have to make the best of it. So, please, quit arguing and let's try to make this work. Okay?"

We both agreed but avoided eye contact.

"Okay." She looked at the time on her phone. "Let's finish this up and find the cabin. I think you're going to really like living out here if you just give it a chance. I mean, come on, you have to admit—the scenery is already beautiful."

"California was beautiful, too," replied Nathan, grabbing a stack of pizzas from the freezer. "I'm just saying..."

She scowled at him. "Seriously?"

He put the pizzas in the cart. "Okay, fine, I'll admit that it's different here. The fresh air, the mountains, all of the greenness. I guess it's cool."

"Thank you. Now, let's grab some Hot Pockets and Pizza Rolls," she said, staring at the case.

I grimaced. "Hot Pockets?"

She motioned her thumb at Nathan. "We need to keep him fed. Those are quick and easy."

It was true, he was always hungry, and once his blood sugar began to drop, grumpier than an old man. Apparently, our dad's family was prone to diabetes and mom predicted we'd both end up getting it someday.

I opened the glass door and began sorting through the Hot Pockets with Nathan directing. Forty-five minutes later, the entire cart was full and Deanna was temporarily forgotten.

"That will be two-hundred-and-forty dollars," said the cashier, snapping her gum.

Mom handed the young woman her credit card. The cashier appraised Nathan as he bagged the groceries. When he finished, she smiled. "Thanks. You didn't have to do that, you know. It's my job."

He shrugged. "That's okay. I don't mind."

"You guys just move here?" she asked, twirling a piece of blonde hair around her index finger. "I haven't seen you around."

I refrained from rolling my eyes. *Here we go again.*

Mom smiled. "We did. Just today, in fact."

"Cool," replied the girl, still checking out Nathan. "See you around."

"Yeah." Nathan began pushing the grocery cart outside without as much as a backwards glance.

Mom and I smiled at each other in amusement. He was clueless sometimes.

We caught up to Nathan outside.

"Let's put the groceries in *your* car, Nathan," Mom said. "Mine is too full already."

"Okay." He turned and veered the cart toward his vehicle.

As we were trying to stuff the food into the back of his Mustang, a soft voice greeted us. "Hi. You must be new in town?"

We all turned around to see a striking redhead getting out of a tall Chevy pickup. She wore a miniscule white sundress, which showed off her toned legs, and dark sunglasses, which I thought was a little odd, considering it was dusk.

Nathan's blue eyes lit up and he grinned. "Yeah, we just pulled into town."

She smiled back, her teeth a pearly white. "I hope you enjoy it here. It's quaint, but there are lots of things to do, especially after dark."

"Good to know," Nathan replied, his voice deeper than usual.

Mom looked at me and we both bit back smiles.

The girl dropped her keys, and after she bent to retrieve them, tossed her curly mass of red hair over her shoulder. It was a simple thing, but it had an immediate effect on Nathan.

"Maybe we'll run into each other sometime?" he said.

"I'm sure we will. It was really nice meeting you," she replied, clearly directing it toward Nathan, who looked like he'd all but forgotten about Deanna.

He nodded. "You, too."

She looked at my mother and me. "See you around."

"Have a good night," Mom replied.

I smiled at her. "Bye."

The girl looked at Nathan one last time before sashaying into the store like some sort of runway model, which she clearly could pass for.

"Wow." I smirked, turning toward my brother. "You can reel your tongue back in now."

"What do you mean?"

I snorted. "Oh, come on, Nathan."

He smiled innocently. "There's nothing wrong with being friendly to strangers, especially when they look like that."

"I think the feeling was mutual," replied Mom, looking at me. "That smile she gave him was enough to light up the entire street."

"How can she resist?" he said cockily. "Heck, I'll bet I'm the best thing that's ever walked into this town."

I sighed. "Don't say that. I'm going to have to side with you on moving back then, if that's the case."

He grinned. "We might be on opposite sides again if the rest of the chicks look anything like her. Maybe I need to give this place a chance."

Mom smiled. "Exactly."

He started packing more groceries into his trunk. "Let's get the rest of this stuff loaded quickly." Nathan glanced up toward the sky, which was growing darker. "I'm starving and it's getting late."

"Me too," I replied, handing him another bag of groceries.

When we had everything in the trunk, Mom gave Nathan the directions to the cabin, which was a few miles past town, and this time, he led the way.

"Finally." I put on my seatbelt as she pulled out of the parking lot. "I just want to get there already."

"Won't be long now." She turned on the radio and scanned through stations until she found a song she

liked. It was a country one, the singer crooning about his tractor.
I snorted. "What in the hell is this?"
"It's Kenny Chesney."
"She thinks my tractor's sexy?" I deadpanned at her, repeating the verse.
"It's catchy, right?" She started singing the words with Kenny as we hit a stoplight.
Noticing there was a cute, college-aged guy in a Jeep next to us, I quickly turned down the song.
Mom frowned. "What are you doing?" She turned it back up.
"Oh, my God." I slunk down in the seat.
Mom laughed at me and then looked at the guy in the Jeep. "What?" she called out and then turned down the music.
"Nice song!" he yelled, without a drip of sarcasm.
"I know, right?" She winked at me. "See,? This town isn't so bad."
"Just their taste in music."
She chuckled. "I'll turn you into a country-song lover yet."
"Don't hold your breath."
"Party pooper." She cranked up the music.

DARKNESS ARRIVED VERY quickly, and in a small town, with very few lights along the roads, it was a little creepy.
Mom frowned. "It's a bitch driving when you don't know exactly where you're going." She craned her neck forward. "I think the turnoff is coming up in another few miles or so. I hope Nathan catches it in time and doesn't overshoot it."
"Knowing him, he probably will," I answered with a smirk. "Especially, if he's on the phone with Deanna again."

"He seemed to forget about her when that redhead made an appearance. She was very pretty."

"Yes, which isn't always a good thing. Girls like that are usually high maintenance. Heck, she's probably *worse* than Deanna."

She grunted. "Yikes, you could be right. She was bad enough."

I stared at her in shock and laughed. "See? You weren't crazy about her either."

Mom gave me a wide-eye look. "I don't know what you're—" She stopped mid-sentence. "Are you kidding me?" she groaned, scowling into the rearview mirror.

I turned to see the flashing lights from a police car. "What, were you speeding or something?"

Mumbling under her breath, Mom pulled over to the side of the road. "No, of course not. You know me, I never speed."

It was true, she was an annoyingly slow driver and Nathan was always giving her crap about it. Even the elderly flipped her off for going too slow sometimes.

Mom rolled down the window as the police officer approached. She immediately handed him her driver's license and insurance information. "I'm sorry, Officer... was I speeding?"

Nathan had noticed the cop, too, and pulled over ahead of us, waiting. He sent me a text message, wondering what was happening. I sent him one back, explaining that I wasn't really sure yet.

"No, but you do have a taillight out," he replied with an easy smile.

My eyes widened as I stared at his white teeth.

What was with this town and their gleaming choppers?

"Oh, no, really?" she answered, biting her lower lip. "Oh, man, I'm sorry. It must have just gone out."

"Yes. Anne Gerard... you must be new in town?" he asked, studying her license.

She smiled. "We are, in fact"—she wagged her thumb at me—"this is my daughter, Nikki, and that's my son, Nathan, ahead of us in the Mustang."

He glanced down at her left hand, which no longer had a wedding ring, and his smile broadened.

"Nice to meet you, ladies, I'm Sherriff Caleb Smith. Welcome to Shore Lake." He handed back her license and puffed out his chest, like Nathan sometimes did when he was trying to look *SWOL*.

I rolled my eyes.

"Thank you," answered my mom with a silly grin on her face.

"Since you have such a lovely smile and you're new in town, I'm just going to give you a warning. Make sure you take care of it as soon as you can, though. Next time I might not be so easy on you."

Mom smiled wider than ever. "I will, thank you, Officer."

He tipped his hat. "It's Sheriff. But my friends call me Caleb. Drive safely now."

"Wow," said Mom after she'd rolled up her window. "Did you see that man's eyes? They were an amazing shade of violet. I don't think I've ever seen anyone with that color of eyes. No wedding ring, either."

I stared at her in disbelief.

She frowned. "What?"

"How can you even..." My voice trailed off.

"Even what? Don't look at me like that, Nikki. There's nothing wrong with making new friends; especially friends who are in law enforcement," she replied with a straight face.

"Well, I guess," I answered, staring into the darkness. Obviously, she was beginning to get a handle on her fears and I should have been relieved, but instead, it only made me... uneasy. She'd just left one cop, and I couldn't see how she would want to try it out with another.

4

WHEN WE FINALLY made it to the cabin, I was stunned. It was two stories high and made of large cedar logs. There were windows everywhere, and a deck that wrapped around the home.

"What do you think?" asked Mom as she parked the car next to Nathan's.

"It's amazing," I replied, opening the car door. "Are you sure this is the right place?"

"It's the right cabin. I saw pictures but wanted to surprise you."

This was no average lakeside cabin; it looked like something you'd see on television. A retreat for the rich and famous.

"This must be worth millions. I can't believe we're staying here," I said, unable to wipe the grin from my face.

"Yes, it's quite extraordinary." She sighed contently. "I'm still in shock that we get to stay here, too. Ernie is a lifesaver."

"He's more like Santa Claus."

"He sure is."

I was mesmerized by how luxurious the place was and couldn't wait to check out the inside. It was possible that Shore Lake wasn't going to suck quite as much as I thought.

She reached into the car and pulled out her cell phone. "I'd better call him once we've unpacked the groceries. Let him know we've made it and how thrilled we are." Her eyes became misty. "You know, I just can't thank him enough for everything he's done."

I agreed with her there. This place was beyond anything we'd ever be able to afford. I knew if it was as extravagant on the inside as it was on the outside, I'd never want to leave.

"All it takes is money, huh?" she said with a wry smile.

"No doubt."

"Ernie mentioned that there's a gazebo and a hot tub in the back. If we ever wanted to entertain, this would definitely be the place to do it," Mom mused.

"Yeah. Tell Nathan. He can throw a party for his new harem."

She snorted.

He got out of the car, his eyes wide as he took in the cabin. "Damn, this place is lit. How in the world did you score something so sweet?"

Mom smiled. "Ernie."

"Look, there's the boathouse," I said, pointing down toward the lake. Even that place looked like it was larger than some of the homes in our old neighborhood.

Nathan nodded in approval. "I hope the weather is nice tomorrow so we can take the boat out." He started walking toward the dock. "I wonder what kind they have..."

"Check later." Mom grabbed her purse. "We need to get this stuff inside."

He sighed and turned around. "Okay. It's probably too dark to see anything now, anyway."

"And the mosquitos are out," I said, swatting at one. "I hope someone packed some bug spray."

"I did." Mom took the keys out of her purse and began walking toward the cabin. "You know, I'm really surprised that there isn't some kind of an alarm on this cabin. I mean, this place is vacant most of the time." She looked over her shoulder at us. "I hope when we get inside, nothing is missing."

"Everyone must trust each other in these parts," I said, following her up the steps to the front door.

"Apparently." She shoved the key into the lock. "Still, if this was my place, I'd have one installed."

I agreed.

She unlocked the door and flipped on the lights. Looking past her, my breath caught in my throat.

Nathan whistled as he followed her inside first. "Damn, this place is tight."

"It's stunning." She smiled. "I'm just… speechless."

I swatted at a bug. "Hey, keep moving. I'm still out here and you're letting all of the mosquitos in."

Mom got out of the way. "Sorry."

I stepped into the great room. It was enormous and had a large soapstone fireplace with a bearskin rug lying near it. Admittedly, it was kind of cheesy, but it certainly added to the effect. Plush, burgundy leather furniture, with hand-carved wooden end tables, sat across from the fireplace. I imagined myself in the oversized chair, reading a book next to a crackling fire, and it made me smile.

Mom pointed out the vaulted ceiling and the rustic chandeliers that warmly lit up the place.

"They're pretty cool. So is the fireplace," Nathan replied. It was built up to the ceiling with natural stone.

"It must have taken weeks to install that. It probably cost as much as our old house to build it, too," Mom replied. "Don't get your dirty shoes on the rug, Nathan."

He moved off it quickly. "Sorry."

"It's okay. I just want to keep everything nice." Mom walked over to the built-in entertainment center and ran her hand over the wood. "Look at the craftsmanship, it must have cost a fortune to have all of this installed. It's made out of walnut. I think."

"Is that expensive?" I asked.

"Oh, yeah."

Nathan sat down on the sofa, closed his eyes, and smiled. "I could definitely get used to this."

Mom walked over and ruffled his hair. "Me, too. The next time I see Ernie, I'm going to plant a huge kiss on his little bald head."

Nathan opened one eye. "Give him one for me, too."

She looked amused. "Oh, so you're finally warming up to us being here?"

He closed his eyes again and smiled. "Mom, seriously, if you're happy, then I'm happy."

"Me, too," I said.

She looked like she was going to cry. "I swear, I have the two best kids in the world."

"Well, *yeah*," Nathan replied. "I've been telling you that for years."

Chuckling, Mom walked over to one of the large glass windows and stared outside. "I just want everything to work out for you and your sister."

"It will." He yawned.

I looked over at the staircase. I couldn't wait to see the rest of the house. "Guys, I'm going to check out the upstairs."

"Pick out a bedroom!" she called as I made it to the top of the stairs. "I don't care which; I hear they're all pretty nice."

"Then I'm calling the bedroom with the king-sized bed if you don't care," I heard Nathan say.

"I get the balcony then!" I hollered down.

"Wait, there's one with a balcony?" he replied.

5

AS IT TURNED OUT, there were several bedrooms on the upper level, two of them with king-sized beds. They were all spacious, with walk-in-closets and attached bathrooms. I chose one with a queen-sized pillow-top bed and a balcony that provided a view of the lake. Although it was rustic, like the lower level, the comforter set was gray and pink, making the bedroom seem a little more feminine. Especially with all the throw pillows. My favorite thing, however, was the built-in bookshelf that took up an entire wall. It was lined with books, many of them very old and some quite new. Nearby was a comfy-looking chaise and a small side-table with a lamp.

"So, what do you think?" Mom asked from the doorway a few seconds later.

I put the book back I'd been looking at and turned to her. "It's awesome. I can't get over it."

Her eyes widened when she saw the bookshelf. "Wow. This is right up our alley."

We both really enjoyed reading.

"Do you want this room?"

She smiled and shook her head. "No, honey. I want you to have it. I will have to borrow a book or two, however."

"There's plenty to choose from."

"I see that." Her eyes scanned the room. "Have you checked out the balcony yet?"

"No." I walked over to the door and opened it. There was a cool breeze outside. Shivering, I pulled my sleeves over my hands. "Brrr."

"It's August. The nights get pretty chilly here this time of the year. I heard that the winters in Montana can be pretty brutal too."

"That's okay. I'm looking forward to having a white Christmas."

She smiled. "Me, too."

I stared out into the distance. It was dark outside, but the reflection of the moon on the water made the lake seem so peaceful. I imagined myself lying in a canoe and staring up at the starlit sky with the waves rocking me to sleep. "I just can't believe this place. If we're dreaming, I never want to wake up."

She linked her arm through mine. "Don't worry, it's real."

We stood there together for a few minutes, both of us gazing at the lake and enjoying the moment. Until my stomach growled.

Mom chuckled. "Goodness, I forgot about how hungry everyone is. Your brother is probably raiding the groceries as we speak. I told him to bring the bags in," she said.

"We'd better get down there before he leaves us with nothing."

"Exactly. That kid is going to eat us out of house-and-home one day."

We went back downstairs, to the gourmet kitchen, and I helped Mom put the rest of the groceries away in the fridge.

"Amazing," I said, admiring the enormous stainless-steel refrigerator. It was twice the size of the one we'd left at home. "I think we'll finally be able to keep enough food in the house to feed Nathan."

Laughing, she took out a frying pan from one of the unpacked boxes. "Who wants cheeseburger sliders?"

Nathan entered the kitchen carrying a bag of groceries. "Did I hear someone say sliders? I'll take as many as you can make. I'm going to pass out if I don't get something to eat soon."

"I'm surprised you're still walking," I said dryly.

"Me too. I'm feeling a little dizzy. No joke." He set the bag down on the counter and opened up the refrigerator. He grabbed a jar of pickles and untwisted the cap. He grinned. "Maybe I'm pregnant?"

"That would explain the moods," I ribbed.

"Ha. Ha. I wouldn't go there. We all know to take cover when you have your period." Before he could get his fingers inside of the jar, Mom stopped him.

"Here." She handed him a fork. "Don't use your fingers."

He grinned sheepishly. "Oh, thanks. I'll put the rest of the groceries away in a second."

"Thank you." She began preparing dinner. "So, is this place incredible, or what?"

"Not too shabby," said Nathan between bites of his pickle. "And it's so quiet, I feel like we're in the middle of nowhere."

"We are," I replied.

Mom began forming hamburger patties. "The next cabin is just a hop, skip, and a jump from here, but you'd never know it's so peaceful."

I grabbed an onion and began cutting it for the burgers. "You did good, Mom. I just can't wait until tomorrow when we get to see it all in the daylight."

Nathan nodded. "Yeah, I'd really like to take the boat out on the lake tomorrow, if that's okay?"

"Sure," she answered. "I can't see why not."

He wiped his hands on his jeans. "Sweet."

She opened the fridge and grabbed the bundle of cheese slices. "I think it would be good for all of us to get out on that lake. I haven't been able to work on my tan all summer."

I snorted. My mom was as white as a ghost and typically burned and peeled, but never really tanned. My brother and I were lucky.

"I'd better not forget my sunglasses then," Nathan joked. "The glow from your skin reflecting off of the lake is sure to be blinding."

"Very funny, wise guy. Just be grateful you can step outside and get a tan within seconds," she said.

"I guess that's one nice thing we inherited from the old man. Everything else awesome was from you," Nathan replied.

"Good save," she said, winking.

AFTER DINNER, I helped her with the dishes and then decided to try out the whirlpool tub.

"I'm taking a bath and then going to bed," I said as we neared the staircase. It had been a long drive, and I was so exhausted, I didn't even feel like unpacking anything just yet.

"Okay." She kissed the top of my head. "I'll see you in the morning."

I glanced over at the boxes near the staircase. "I'd better find some of my things first."

"If you need any help, let me know," Mom replied.

"Okay."

A moving company had dropped off our belongings earlier in the day and I found some of my own boxes very quickly. After carrying them to my room, I grabbed a towel and the fluffy white robe my mom had given me for Christmas last year. As I was about to walk into my bathroom to start the tub, there was a soft knock.

"Yeah?"

My brother opened the door. "Hey, I'm sorry about snapping at you earlier. You were right." He gave me a sheepish grin. "I guess I was being a little bit of an asshole."

"Don't worry, I'm used to it."

His smile fell. He folded his arms across his chest. "Well, you were kind of a bitch too, you know."

"Cause and effect."

"So, it's my fault?" he replied dryly.

"Your words not mine."

"If you're out of Midol, I can give you a lift into town tomorrow to buy some more."

I threw my hairbrush at him. It missed and hit the wall next to the door.

He snorted. "You throw like a girl."

"I'll show you 'girl'." I picked up my curling iron and raised it in the air. "Leave before I give you ringlets! I swear to God, I'll make you pretty!"

He fluttered his lashes. "Can you do my nails and give me a facial too? Hey, I know—we should have a spa night!"

I broke down and started laughing. "You are such a freak."

"No need to be jealous. You're my twin and kind of a freak, too."

"Lucky me."

He smiled. "Night, Nik. I'll see you in the morning."

"Okay, goodnight."

After he left, I grabbed my things and stepped into the bathroom, locking the door behind me. When I turned back around, I smiled.

This was all mine.

Talk about a luxurious bathroom. There was even a large panoramic window surrounding the Jacuzzi with a view of the lake. Although it was dark and I couldn't see much of anything outside, I imagined during the day, it was incredible.

I walked to the large tub and turned on the water. Sitting on the edge, I watched it rise slowly, wondering how many gallons I'd be using before it covered the jets entirely. It was enormous, enough to hold up to two or three people.

Looking forward to getting into it myself, I stood back up and opened the new mango-scented spa bath gift set my mom had given me. It included a candle, but I didn't have a lighter on me, so I dimmed the lights. When the water was high enough, I removed my clothes and pulled my hair back into a ponytail.

Stepping into the tub, I groaned in pleasure and sunk into the warm bath. I laid my head against the pillow and closed my eyes.

Music. I need music.

Remembering that I left my phone in the bedroom, I stood up and was about to grab a towel, when something caught the corner of my eye. I turned my head toward the fogged-up window and my heart stopped as a set of fiery-red eyes stared back at me. I froze in fear, every hair standing on end as I stood frozen in horror. When I finally found my voice, I screamed, and whatever it was, quickly shot away.

"Mom!" I shrieked, trying not to slip on the wet floor. I grabbed my robe and skidded out of the bathroom as quickly as possible.

"What is it?" she cried, bursting through the door, also wearing a robe.

Trembling, I pointed toward the bathroom. "Someone was watching me from the window in there."

Her eyes widened. "Are you sure?"

"Yes, I'm sure!"

"I'll be right back." With an angry look on her face, she left and returned shortly with the baseball bat she now kept in her room. "Let's go and have a look."

With my heart pounding in my chest, I followed her into the bathroom, half expecting someone to jump out of the shadows. She kept the light switch off and moved toward the window.

"Do you see anything?" I whispered, standing behind her. After opening the door, the windows had defogged and we appeared to be surrounded by nothing but darkness.

Sighing, she lowered the bat. "No."

I wasn't so sure. Something was still out there. I could feel it in my bones. "Are you sure?"

Her forehead wrinkled. "Yes, I'm sure. I also don't see how anyone could be watching you from this height, Nikki."

I was frustrated that she didn't believe me. "Mom, someone or something was *there*. Watching me. I'm not lying."

"I didn't say you were." Her eyes softened; she touched my cheek. "Baby, it's been a long day and we're in the middle of the woods. You probably saw an owl flying by, or maybe even a bat. Don't be frightened."

"But—"

"Think about it, a peeping Tom would need wings to get up here."

She was obviously right. My bedroom *was* several feet from the ground, and truthfully, I really wasn't sure what I'd seen. Obviously, it had to be some kind of animal. "I guess that's possible."

Mom held out a hand to me. "Come here and see for yourself. Look how far up we really are."

I looked outside and common sense told me that we were too high for any person to be looking in.

I closed my eyes. "Yeah, okay, maybe it *was* just a stupid bat or something."

"Honey, you're obviously very tired. Why don't you go to bed and get a good night's sleep? I'll bet tomorrow you'll be laughing about this."

Nathan came to the door, wearing his blue flannel pajama pants. "Is everything okay in here?"

"Everything's fine," she answered with another reassuring smile. "Nikki just saw a huge bird or something outside and it scared the hell out of her."

Nathan's eyebrows shot up. "Seriously? You know, I thought I saw one too when I was in my room watching TV. It freaked the shit out of me."

I turned to see her reaction.

"What?" she asked, staring at both of us, amused. "Come on... it's some kind of bird. You know, there's no possible way a living person could stand outside of your bedroom windows and look in. Unless Spider-Man is vacationing in Montana and has decided to scale this particular cabin to check us out. You two are wigging out over nothing."

"Still, I think we should take a look outside." Nathan turned and began walking away. "That thing had red eyes. I don't know of any bird that has those."

"Wait!" my mom hollered. She picked up the bat and charged after him. "Don't go out there without this!"

And she thought I was being paranoid?

I followed them downstairs. When we reached the landing, I watched as Nathan switched on the outdoor lights and threw open the front door.

"Be careful!" I hollered, staying back. There was no way I was going outside, harmless bird or not.

Mom hesitantly followed Nathan while I wrapped my arms around myself, trying to remain calm.

This is crazy, I thought when they closed the door behind them. We're probably overreacting. I wondered if it really was some kind of large bird checking both of us out. Maybe an owl or eagle?

But with *red* eyes? Even Nathan had mentioned seeing them.

I chewed on my lower lip and stared toward the dark windows, suddenly wondering if someone or something was watching me from the other side. It made the hair stand up on the back of my neck. I leaped toward the windows and began lowering the wooden blinds across all four large plated windows. Once they were all covered, I took a step back, my mind still reeling a mile a minute. I began to pace as the anxiety quickly built up again. I was definitely wigging out, just like she'd said. I started imaging things like Sasquatches and aliens, freaking myself out until I felt like I was almost to the point of hyperventilating.

Jesus, Nikki, chill the hell out.

Frustrated, I went back over to the sofa and sat down, tapping my foot nervously. Seconds later, my brother stormed through the front door, followed by my mom, whose face was as pale as the moon. He picked up the phone and started dialing.

My stomach tightened when I noticed the troubled look on Nathan's face. "Okay, what's going on?"

Nathan raised his hand to silence me and then began speaking, his voice strangled. "Hello? Yes, I'd like to report a dead body."

6

THREE HOURS LATER, the dead body, which they'd found near the dock, was examined, bagged, and finally taken away.

"Well," said Sheriff Caleb Smith, who was standing on the porch. "It looks like it's the teenage girl who's been missing for a few weeks, Tina Johnson."

"What happened to her?" I asked, staring at him. He was taller than I'd thought, standing well over six-foot, with dark hair that hung just below his collar. He had almost perfectly chiseled face, except for his nose, which was a little large. I had to admit, though, for an older guy, he was handsome.

"I guess I could share a little of that with you, considering you found her on your property," he replied.

My mother cleared her throat. "Before you get into all of that, would you like to come in and have a cup of coffee, Sheriff?"

He grinned widely and stepped inside. "Thanks. Don't worry about the coffee, though. I really need to be leaving soon."

"So, was she murdered?" asked Nathan, still freaked out about finding her bloated body sticking out of the water. He'd described it so many times to me that I could see the image in my head as if I'd actually been there.

The sheriff shook his head. "I don't think so. She had a history of drinking and left a party pretty intoxicated at the time she went missing. She may have simply fallen into the water and drowned. There will be an autopsy, however, so we'll know more later."

Nathan, who watched a lot of crime shows on television, crossed his arms over his chest. "So, there were no witnesses? Nobody at the party actually saw her leave?"

The sheriff put his hand on the wall and leaned against it. "No. That particular party got a little out of hand and we ended up arresting a few minors for intoxication that night. It was an ugly mess."

Mom clicked her tongue and sighed. "Goodness, what a horrible thing for her parents. I can't imagine what it's been like for them."

He nodded, looking very somber. "Just like us, they've been frantically searching for her all over this town, and the next ones over. Well, at least they'll have some closure now."

"How tragic. I can't possibly imagine how I'd cope in their situation," she said.

He nodded. "I agree."

I was still freaking out a little. "So, you think it was an accident but you're not certain?"

"I'm about ninety-nine percent sure that's what it was. I really wouldn't let this get to you. This is a peaceful town and I know everyone living here. They're all good people."

"But what if she was murdered by someone driving through who may have picked her up?" I asked.

"Oh, Nikki. Don't jump to conclusions," Mom admonished, throwing me a look.

"I understand your concern. I don't think she was hitchhiking, though. She was last seen by the lake.

Someone thought she might have gone skinny-dipping," the sheriff said.

Nathan frowned. "Alone?"

"Yeah. It sounded that way," he answered.

"That's sad," Nathan replied.

Sheriff Caleb sighed. "Honestly, I don't know exactly what happened, but my gut is telling me it wasn't murder. So, don't let this incident scare you away. If I thought you were in any kind of real danger, I'd tell you."

"I believe you, Sheriff," Mom replied and looked at us. "Alcohol can make people do crazy things. We all know that."

She was obviously talking about our father. Nathan and I nodded in agreement.

Mom turned back to the sheriff. "Are you sure you wouldn't like a cup of coffee? It'll just take a minute to brew."

"No, Anne, but thanks again for the offer." He straightened up and patted his pockets as if searching for his keys. "I'd better get going; my daughter's expecting me home soon."

"You have children?" she asked.

He smiled proudly. "A daughter, Celeste. She just graduated from high school."

Mom's eyes sparkled with interest. "Oh, you're a single parent?"

What in the hell was going on with her? I thought. She wasn't acting like herself. It was unsettling.

He nodded. "Yes, we've been alone now for quite a few years."

"That must be difficult. Being a single parent, that is. It's challenging with normal hours. I could only imagine what you're going through, with such crazy ones," Mom said.

"It's not too bad. It's just Celeste, and she's... fairly manageable. You... *you* have twins. That must be quite a handful."

She waved her hand. "Not really. They're pretty good kids."

He smiled. "Good, then they won't have to see much of me."

Mom burst out laughing as if he'd said *the* funniest thing she'd ever heard.

Nathan and I looked at each other. Even he noticed she was acting strangely.

"Oh, hell, I'm just kidding. Most of the other kids around here are pretty well-behaved, as well," said the sheriff.

Except for Tina, apparently.

"Good, then I can relax when these two start meeting other kids in town and go out at night," she replied.

He tilted his head and leaned forward. "I wouldn't go that far. They *are* still teenagers."

Nathan and I looked at each other and rolled our eyes.

Mom sighed. "So very true. Well, thanks for making it out here so quickly. We were all pretty shaken up."

His face turned grim. "I'm sure. What a horrible experience for your first night in Shore Lake, too. I'm sorry you had to go through this."

Mom nodded. "It was certainly an eventful evening. Crazy, huh?"

"I'd say." He put his hat on. "I'd better get going. I hope the next time we meet it's under much better circumstances."

She followed him to the door. "Me, too. Goodnight, Sheriff."

"Caleb," he said softly, looking down at her.

Her cheeks flushed. "Goodnight, Caleb."

It was actually early morning, but Mom and Caleb didn't seem to notice. They were too busy staring at each other with their lonely, middle-aged hormones.

"Goodbye, Sheriff," said Nathan, yawning.

"Yeah, see you," I added with a wave, hoping he'd just *leave* already.

Caleb smiled once more with his gleaming white teeth and then *finally* walked out the front door.

"He's such a nice man," Mom said with a stupid grin on her face. "It's so refreshing to know this town has a great guy like him patrolling the streets."

I grunted. "You hardly know him." I got up from the couch. "For all we know, he's a total jerk and this could all be an act. Look at Dad. He was a freaken cop, too."

Both my mom and brother stared at me in surprise.

I scowled. "Don't look at me like that. You know it's true. You should know more than anyone, Mom."

Her eyebrows knitted together. "Oh, for Heaven's sake, Nikki, don't be so quick to judge other people."

"Yeah, chill out," Nathan said. "I thought he was nice."

I started walking up the steps to my bedroom, exhausted and wanting to forget about the last couple of hours. I didn't know what was more troubling—the dead body or the way my mother had been flirting with the sheriff. "Whatever, I'm going to bed."

"She's just being a crab-ass," said Nathan. "I'll pick her up some Midol later today."

"I heard that!" I hollered.

They both chuckled.

I SLEPT UNTIL almost noon. Mom was already up, drinking coffee and working on her computer, when I padded downstairs in my bare feet.

"Morning," I said, pouring some coffee for myself. Normally, I wasn't a coffee drinker, but I really needed something stronger than orange juice to perk me up. Especially after the crazy evening we'd had.

"Good morning," she answered with a beaming smile. She was always a morning person no matter how late she stayed up.

"Where's Nathan?"

"I'm not sure. I think he might be outside by the boat. We were thinking about taking it out on the lake within the hour."

"Okay." I yawned. "I'll eat something and get ready."

"Good."

Nathan stepped into the house through the sliding glass door. He grinned when he looked at me. "Look who finally crawled out of bed. Mom was getting worried about you."

"I couldn't sleep last night. Even after the cops left," I said.

"It's okay. Don't let him get to you," Mom said, giving Nathan a dirty look. "And I wasn't worried about her, Nathan. Don't make her feel guilty."

He snickered.

I took a drink of coffee and walked over to the window. The skies were blue and it looked like a beautiful day. Then I thought about the dead girl from last night again and shuddered.

"Did you really actually find her in the water?" I asked. The idea of swimming in the lake when there'd been a floating body in it was harrowing. I seriously doubted I could even put my foot in the water.

"Why?"

I could tell from her expression that she knew where this was going.

I shrugged. "It's just kind of gross to think about swimming in it. Don't you think?"

"Don't worry, Nikki," Nathan replied. "That lake is so freaken big, I'm sure there are plenty of other bodies lost somewhere beneath the surface. People still swim in it all the time."

I shot him a dirty look. "That's gross."

Mom groaned. "Thanks, Nathan. Listen, people drown and it's just a fact of life. I'm sure every lake has stories of people disappearing in it, including the ones *you've* swam in the past."

I walked toward the staircase with my coffee. "That doesn't make it sound any more enticing. I think I'll just enjoy the view on the lake and try not to think about what's *under* it."

"Just make sure you're ready to go in an hour!" hollered Nathan as I headed up the stairs. "Or we're leaving you behind."

7

AN HOUR-AND-A-HALF LATER, I'd changed into my new orange and pink bikini, and we were racing across the lake in a twenty-five-foot Stingray. Nathan was grinning from ear to ear; Mom was also smiling while desperately trying to hold her straw sunhat onto her head. Unfortunately, all I could think about the girl in the lake. I just couldn't shake the horror of knowing there'd been a body near the cabin we were now staying. Accident, or not, it was creepy. I had to admit, the fact that my mother and brother were able to push it aside was a disturbing, too. It was almost like they'd forgotten all about it.

"This is sweet!" yelled Nathan over the motor as his light brown hair whipped in the wind. "There's hardly anyone out here and we have the entire lake to ourselves!"

It was true, but it was also early in the week. From the look of all the boats docked near the shoreline, this place was probably a madhouse on the weekends.

Nathan slowed down after crossing the entire lake and set the anchor. He smiled eagerly and rubbed his hands together. "Okay, I'm going for a swim. Who's with me?"

"Sounds good, but not me." Mom pulled out a book from her tote. "You know what I'm going to do—read and work on my tan."

I handed her some sunscreen. "Not without this. You'll be a lobster tonight as it is."

"Yeah. You know me too well." She began rubbing some of the coconut scented lotion into her skin.

Nathan removed his T-shirt. "Coming in, twerp?"

"Quit calling me that," I snarled. "Maybe later I'll come in and drown *you*."

"Challenge accepted. I'd like to see you try. *Twerp*!" He dove into the dark water. When he surfaced, he yelled, "Wow, it's really nice! Come on out, Nikki. Don't be such a wuss!"

The sun was shining, it was already eighty degrees, and as I stared at him in the water, I had to admit, it did look *very* enticing.

Maybe I was overreacting...

I let out a long sigh and stood up. I lifted the white beach dress over my head and dove into the cool water.

"See," Nathan said when I popped my head back out. "It's not so bad."

I wiped some water away from my eyes and smiled. "Yeah, I guess not." It also didn't hurt that we were on the other side of the lake from where the girl had been found. That was comforting.

A small fishing boat was trolling toward us and I strained to see who was driving it, half expecting Sheriff white-tooth. Something told me that we hadn't seen the last of him, especially by the way he'd been ogling Mom. Even today in her bikini, she'd caught the attention of a couple fishermen we'd passed by on the lake. Heck, I couldn't deny the fact that she looked pretty fit for someone reaching forty.

"Hey," shouted Nathan at the young man who'd stopped his boat next to ours. "How's it going?"

The dark-haired guy looked about our age, maybe a little older. He wore black sunglasses and blue and white striped swim trunks. He had a nice body and was pretty tan, too. I secretly hoped I didn't have any smudged mascara on my wet face.

"Pretty good. Nice boat!" he hollered back.

Nathan smiled. "It's not ours, but thanks."

The stranger removed his sunglasses and returned the smile. "I'm Duncan. You guys vacationing out here?"

"No," answered Mom. "We're renting a cabin on the other side of the lake."

He nodded. "There are more than enough cabins available on this lake, that's for sure."

"Really? Why is that?" I asked, feeling tense again. *Were people moving away?*

He stared at me for a minute and shrugged. "I just meant that some of these cabins are only seasonal homes, so many of the owners rent them out during the year when they're not in use."

"Oh," I replied. That made sense.

Mom grinned at Duncan. "I'm Anne, by the way. And those two in the water are Nikki and Nathan."

He smiled back. "Nice meeting you all."

"You too," replied Nathan.

"Do you live close by then, Duncan?" Mom asked.

He nodded. "I live with my dad on the north side of the lake. He owns the boat repair shop over there, and our place is right next to it."

"Cool," said Nathan. "I suppose you get to see a lot of kickass boats coming through there."

"Definitely. My dad's is the only repair shop nearby, so he's pretty busy, even with my help. Because the lake is so big and there's money on it, we definitely get some nice little yachts coming in for repairs."

I swam back over to our boat and climbed up the steps while Nathan and Duncan continued talking boats. As Mom handed me a towel, I noticed Duncan stealing glances my way. When our eyes suddenly met, he quickly looked away.

"So, what do you guys do for fun here, other than fishing?" asked Nathan.

Duncan cleared his throat. "Actually, the town is having their annual end of summer barbeque this weekend at Turtle Beach. It's on the northern side of the lake, too. I'm sure they'll have tons of food and games. Then, at night, they'll launch the fireworks. They do it every year."

Mom's eyes lit up. "Sounds like fun. We'd better not miss that shindig."

He nodded. "It's a pretty big deal. Almost everyone in town will be there."

"Will you?" I blurted out unexpectedly. I surprised everyone, even myself.

Duncan stared at me for a moment and smiled. "I wasn't planning on it, but it's starting to sound more interesting."

I could feel my face burning and it wasn't from the sun. "I, um... I just think it would be nice for Nathan to have someone to hang out with. He gets so bored, sometimes..."

"She's right," replied Nathan, smirking at me, as if he knew I was back-peddling. "I need a partner-in-crime. I'm bored out of my mind now that we're in a new town and I have no friends to raise hell with."

Duncan laughed. "I don't know much about raising hell, but if you're bored, you should stop by the shop later today. We just took in this mint Bluewater yacht that is *incredible*. I might even know someone with the keys who could give you a private tour."

"Nice! I might have to take you up on that," Nathan said, his face brightening.

Just then, a couple flew by us on a pair of jet-skis and Duncan turned to watch them, giving me another opportunity to check him out. I had to admit that he was not only cute, but had nicely sculpted pecs and arms. It was obvious he worked out when he wasn't working on boats. Before I had a chance to look away, he turned back and caught me staring. I immediately looked away, hoping my face wasn't as red as Nathan's trunks.

Mom, who was watching me, looked amused. "What's wrong, Nikki?"

"Nothing," I answered, a little too sharply.

She smiled.

"Your face looks red," said Nathan, with another knowing smile. "Better use some sunscreen."

I shot him an angry look and he turned away, chuckling.

"I suppose I should get back to the marina. By the way, you ladies are invited, too, of course," said Duncan.

"Thanks," said Mom, "but maybe another time. I have too much to do this afternoon."

"No problem. I'll be around the shop all evening. Hope to see you there." Duncan's eyes drifted toward me.

I smiled, my stomach fluttering with butterflies.

"Catch you later," Nathan said.

"Sounds good." He started the engine and was gone.

"That's cool," Nathan said as he got back on the boat after Duncan left. "Now I can check out some nice boats while Nikki checks out Duncan."

My eyes narrowed. "Very funny."

He smiled. "Come on, I saw the way you were drooling over him!"

"I was not!" I snapped. "I was just checking his boat out."

He threw his head back and laughed. "Right! Since when do you have an interest in boats?"

"I always have…" I sputtered.

My mom smiled and added her two cents. "Actually, I also noticed you were checking out more than the boat."

"Whatever. You guys are seeing things. Anyway, you both should talk, what, about that redhead in the parking lot yesterday, and... Sheriff White Strips?"

Mom looked confused. "Sheriff *White Strips?*"

Nathan nodded. "Yeah, Caleb. His teeth were whiter than your pasty skin, mom. Bleached white."

"I didn't notice," she replied.

"That's because they glowed so brightly, you probably couldn't get a good look at his face," replied Nathan.

"What do you mean? She couldn't take her eyes *off* of his face," I said dryly.

She frowned. "What's with the attitude?"

Sighing, I looked away. I felt a little guilty but couldn't shake off the irritation I was feeling.

Maybe I did need Midol.

Nathan started the engine. He grabbed his bottle of water and took a swig. "I say we go back to the cabin now. I'm starving."

"Sounds good," Mom replied. "I know I've got plenty to do."

Nathan set his water into the cup-holder, turned on the engine, and we started back across the lake. A few seconds later, he grinned like a little kid and told us to hold on.

I grabbed the handle next to my seat, right as he punched it down, and we took off across the lake. I squealed in delight as we sped over the calm waters, the wind practically blowing my hair dry as we flew. Soon, we were near our neck of the woods and I pulled my beach-dress over my bathing suit. As we slowed down, I noticed a middle-aged woman sitting on her dock, fishing. She smiled and raised her hand in greeting.

"Must be our neighbor." Mom waved back. "Ernie mentioned that she was recently widowed. I think he said her name was Abigail. Very nice woman, I guess.

Maybe it would be a good idea if I stopped by later and said hello."

I stared at the woman and nodded. "I would. She's probably sad and lonely."

She nodded. "I'm sure."

Nathan docked the boat and we helped him secure it to the posts.

"That should be good enough for now," he said, testing the ropes. "I'll leave it out here in case we want to take it out again later."

I stood up and looked down into the brown water. "So, um, it must be pretty deep right here." We were at the farthest end of the dock, several feet from the shoreline.

"Yeah." Nathan grabbed his shirt from the boat. "That's why they built the dock this distance from the shore. It's safer for the boat if the lake ever gets too low."

The water was so murky-looking and I wondered if there really were any more bodies floating around in the lake. I imagined someone's dead eyes staring up at me from below the surface and could barely breathe.

Crap, I was having another panic attack.

"I'll meet you guys on shore," I said, stepping up onto the dock quickly.

"Are you okay?" called my mom.

"Just a little too much sun," I shouted back as I raced toward the cabin, wanting to put as much distance between myself and the water as possible. When I made it to the porch, I closed my eyes and took a couple deep breaths.

Nathan appeared a short time later. "Hey."

I smiled weakly. "Hey."

He stared at me with concern. "You're really freaked out about that girl, aren't you?"

"Well, yeah. Aren't you?"

He sighed. "I'm trying to forget about it. She obviously screwed up and made a huge mistake the night of the party, paying for it with her life. But I'm not going to dwell on it, and neither should you. Hell, you didn't even see the girl, I discovered her. I should be the one freaking out about it."

"I know," I said softly. "It just really got to me, I guess."

He put an arm around my shoulder. "I get it. It was creepier than hell. But you have to let it go. Or mom will send you to a shrink, which, actually, she should have done a long time ago."

I pushed him away. "Ha-ha."

Mom met us on the porch and took out her keys. Her face as already starting to get pink from the sun. "Whew, it's getting so hot out here. Thank goodness for air conditioning."

"Summer's almost over. Then you'll be complaining about the cold," Nathan replied.

"Yeah, they get negative temperatures here in Montana," I added.

She shrugged. "That's when the fireplace will come in handy. Anyway, I'm looking forward to the colder temperatures and using it."

"Me, too," Nathan said. "I'd better learn how to chop wood, I guess."

"It's a gas fireplace," she replied.

Nathan looked disappointed. "Oh."

We stepped inside and he dropped the boat keys onto an end table. "Nikki, go get dressed and we'll drive into town to check things out. I need to start looking for a job, anyway."

"Okay. I should try and find one, too," I replied. I'd worked at a boutique back in California, and had a little bit of money saved for a car. I needed a lot more, however, to purchase something reliable.

"Good idea. We'll go check out your boyfriend's boat repair shop afterward," he said with a smirk.

I rolled my eyes. "Okay, Wise-ass. You're just full of jokes today."

Mom, who'd been checking her voicemail, started smiling. She ended the call and stared at us. "Guess who asked me to dinner?"

"Sheriff Snaggletooth?" I replied.

Her smile fell. "That's not fair, Nikki. Like I said before, he seems like a very nice man."

I wanted to ask her how she could even think about dating anyone after the volatile relationship she'd had with our dad. But then, I began to wonder if maybe it was part of the healing process. She'd been seeing a counselor and it was possible that he'd encouraged her to try and trust other men.

"You going for it?" asked Nathan, not looking too worried about it.

She tapped her fingers on the banister. "Oh, I don't know. I'm not looking for anything right now, obviously, but as I said before—it never hurts to get in good with the town's sheriff. Maybe I'll just invite him over to our house tonight for dinner. Can you pick up a couple of steaks in town, Nathan?"

He nodded. "But if you want wine, you're on your own."

She snorted. "That's the last thing I need, to get tipsy in front of someone so highly respected."

"Just because he's a cop doesn't mean he doesn't drink alcohol." Nathan smirked. "And if you get too out of hand, he could always handcuff you."

Mom laughed. "Oh, I never thought of that. That could be fun."

I cringed. "T.M.I." I started climbing the staircase.

"Oh, Nikki, I can't wait until the love bug bites you in the butt. I am going to tease the crap out of you," she replied.

"Don't hold your breath. That's not happening anytime soon," I said.

She grinned again. "We'll see."

"Be ready in thirty minutes, Twerp," called Nathan. "We'll go cruising."

8

I TOOK A quick shower and changed into a dark blue halter sundress and white sandals. I pulled my hair into a messy bun and applied mascara to my lashes and a little lip gloss.

Mom smiled at me when I entered the kitchen. "Look at you. You look so pretty."

I looked down at my dress and shrugged. "Oh, it was one of the few things already unpacked. Besides, if I'm going to go looking for a job, I should probably leave my flip-flops and cut-offs back here."

"Good idea." She kissed the top of my head. "Don't break too many hearts in town."

"Ha-ha, Mom. Very funny," I replied, although I did feel sort of pretty in the new dress.

Nathan was polishing up his Mustang when I found him outside. The red paint gleamed in the sun when he was finished.

"What do you think? Chic magnet?" he asked, staring proudly at his car.

"I guess."

"Actually, I was talking about me," he joked. Grinning, he flexed his muscles and did some poses.

I smirked. "You're such a dork."

"More like… beefcake," he replied, trying to make me laugh with some of the faces he was making.

Amused, I shook my head. "Where do you come up with this stuff? Sometimes I can't believe we're twins."

"Neither can I... although we're both pretty damn good looking." He stopped flexing. "By the way, don't take offense if I ask you to duck down while the *ladies* are scoping me out today. With my luck they'll think we're together."

"Right."

He gave me a crooked smile. "Maybe you could just ride in the back?"

I shoved him playfully and then got into the car.

"Mind if I play some 90s music?"

I rolled down the window. "Go for it."

After he found something we both liked, we took our time driving into town, enjoying the scenery.

"Hear from Deanna yet today?"

He grimaced. "Yeah. She called freaking out again. I just don't know what to do about her. I mean, the more I think about it, the more I realize that I'm tired of the drama. Then I look at this town we've moved to and I think about all of the possibilities."

I smiled. "You mean all of the chicks?"

"Of course."

I shook my head at my brother, who was so predictable.

"Okay, keep your eyes peeled for something interesting," said Nathan, brushing his bangs away from his eyes.

"Chicks or jobs?"

"Both."

I laughed.

AS WE ENTERED the town, I pointed right away to a diner called Ruth's. "Let's stop in there and see if they're hiring."

"Good idea. I'm hungry again, anyway."

Nathan pulled into the parking lot and we went inside. A few seconds later we were seated by a frazzled-looking waitress. It was only three in the afternoon, but the place was jam-packed.

"Here are your menus," the woman said. "I'm not your server, but we're short staffed today. So, we're helping each other out."

"No problem," we said in unison.

The waitress smiled. "You two make such a cute couple."

Nathan and I grimaced.

"There goes my appetite. We're brother and sister," Nathan explained.

The woman looked embarrassed. "Oh, I'm sorry. I'll get your server."

"Don't worry about it," he replied, smiling again. "It's an honest mistake."

"Uh, well. I'll send Amy over." She took off.

"Can people not see that we're twins?"

"Maybe we should start dressing the same," I joked. "You know, like Mom used to try doing when we were little."

Nathan smiled. "Maybe. I'd look damn good in a sundress."

I chuckled.

Our waitress appeared with two glasses of water. She was blonde with light blue eyes and a warm smile. "Hi, I'm Amy. I'll be your server today."

"Nice to meet you," Nathan said, his face brightening. "And just so you know, we're brother and sister."

She laughed. "Okay?"

I looked around and saw the other waitress running around and filling coffee cups. "You wouldn't be hiring, would you?"

"Actually, funny you should ask, we're short staffed. Especially at night," she said.

"Really? We just moved into town and are looking for jobs. Could you please get me an application? And a Caesar salad?" I handed her back the menu. "Just put it on his tab."

Nathan snorted.

She laughed. "Okay, so anything to drink?"

"Just the water," I replied. "I'll go easy on him."

Nathan stared down at his menu. "How are the burgers here, Amy?"

"Oh, they're very good. That's why this place is always so busy. That and the fact that we're the only diner open twenty-four hours."

He smiled. "I'll take your word for it, then." He closed the menu and handed it to her. "I'd like a bacon double cheeseburger, an order of onion rings, and a chocolate milkshake."

She smiled back. "Hope you're hungry because they serve big portions here."

That's when Nathan turned on the charm. He leaned forward and smiled. "You know what... I already like this place, sis. Nice portions and even nicer waitresses. What more could a guy ask for?"

Amy blushed. She *was* very pretty, and I had to admit, Nathan was a good-looking guy himself. Obviously, he knew it, too. I wish I felt as comfortable as he did around the opposite sex. I usually clammed up and started sweating around the guys I was attracted to. Nathan was Joe Cool.

"I'll be back with your malt and water in just a moment," she said softly before she walked away.

"I guess Deanna is beginning to fade from your memory as the day progresses," I mused.

His face became serious. "Not really. I mean, there will always be a special place in my heart for her, but

I've decided to keep my options open. I'm young and shouldn't be tying myself down to one girl. Especially one who's a few hundred miles away."

I folded my hands and nodded. "That's why I'm not going to waste time lusting after any guys in this town. I don't want anything holding me back from college."

"You don't have to get serious with anyone here," he said. "You can still go out with guys and have some fun."

I shrugged. "Maybe." Duncan's face popped into my head. "We'll see."

Amy returned with his milkshake and handed me an application.

"Um, if I were you, I'd only request hours during the day or early evening."

"Why?" I asked, puzzled. She'd just mentioned that they were hiring for evenings, which I'd have a better shot at getting. Plus, I'd be starting school soon.

She looked around nervously and then whispered, "It's too dangerous around here at night."

Nathan raised his eyebrows. "What do you mean by dangerous?"

"Amy!" hollered a guy behind the counter, who I assumed was the cook because of his uniform. "Order's up! They're waiting!"

"Sorry, I can't talk about it now," she mumbled. "Just take my word for it. It's not safe."

Then she left us both staring at each other in surprise.

I bit the side of my lower lip. "Wow, first a dead body in the lake and now this? What the hell?"

He waved his hand, brushing it off. "Oh, it might be nothing. Maybe she's talking about drunk drivers or something. I'm sure there's not a lot to do in a town like this but drink and drag race."

"I don't know, but I'll take her word for it. I'd prefer to work during the day, anyway. At least until school starts."

"It's your call. I wouldn't take what she said seriously, though."

Not knowing what to believe, I finished the application just as our food arrived.

"I can take this and give it to the owner if you'd like. She'll be in later this evening," Amy said.

"Thanks." I leaned forward. "So, what did you mean earlier about it being dangerous around here at night?"

Her eyes darted around the restaurant again and I had this feeling like she was genuinely scared. Finally she cleared her throat and mumbled, "I didn't mean anything by it. Just forget I said anything."

At that moment I noticed the diner was unusually quiet and I had the impression that some of the other customers were listening to our conversation. I decided it would be best just to drop the subject.

I raised my voice. "Oh. Well, yeah, if you could give the application to whoever does the hiring, I'd really appreciate it."

She nodded and then stepped away. I immediately noticed that the volume of the diner rose again, and I stared at Nathan curiously.

"Okay, kind of weird," he said under his breath. "Must be a small town thing?"

"Must be," I said, picking up my fork.

We finished our food and Nathan left a big tip for Amy, who was so busy she could barely make it back to the table to refill our glasses.

"You dropped something," called Amy as we were leaving the diner. Before I could respond, she handed me a folded-up note and hurried away.

"What was that all about?" Nathan asked as we walked to the car.

I put my sunglasses on. "Don't know. We'll read it in the car."

When we got into the Mustang, I immediately opened the note and read it out loud. "Lock your doors at night and don't invite any strangers inside." A shiver ran up my spine. I turned to Nathan. "Okay, now *that's* really freaky."

Nathan's cell phone began to ring before he could respond. "It's Mom," he said, answering it.

I could hear them talking about her date with the sheriff and then he hung up.

"I guess it's going to be a late dinner, so we don't have to be home for a few hours. The sheriff won't be at our place until after nine."

I smirked. "I bet. If it's dangerous here at night, he's probably super busy."

"Listen," Nathan replied as we pulled out of the parking lot. "I wouldn't go blowing everything out of proportion. It's possible that Amy was friends with that dead girl and doesn't trust anyone right now. Or maybe, she's a little crazy."

I sighed. "Or maybe, she's just worried about us. You have to admit that finding a dead body, practically on our doorstep, isn't the best housewarming gift."

"Since the sheriff is coming to dinner tonight, why don't we just ask him about it? He'd certainly know if there was something wicked happening around here after dark."

"Maybe. Don't you think it's odd that she feels comfortable enough to date someone already?"

"Nah. I think she just needs to feel safe and he obviously does that for her."

"Maybe." It made sense.

"It's just a date. They're not getting hitched or anything."

"I guess."

"Hey, that must be Duncan's old man's shop," Nathan said, slowing the car down.

I looked up and noticed a large boat marina with a big sign that read "Sonny's Boat Repairs." Nathan pulled into the parking lot and we both got out.

"Wow, check out all of those boats," pointed Nathan, his face lighting up. "Oh man, I think I just had an orgasm."

I rolled my eyes. "Thanks for sharing."

There was a fenced-in storage area for some of the smaller boats not docked at the marina. On the other side was the repair shop.

"I'd like to get myself an old Carver after I find a job," he said as we walked toward the shop's entrance. "I hear you can get one relatively inexpensive and fix it up."

Nathan, like our father, always loved boats. In fact, we used to own a twenty-four-foot Bayliner before my parents split up. Then they had to sell the boat and he'd been bummed out ever since.

"Hey!" called Duncan, coming toward us. He'd changed into a T-shirt, advertising the shop, and faded blue jeans. "You made it."

Nathan grinned. "Yeah. Now that we're here, I have to admit, I'm jealous. You're surrounded by some pretty lit boats."

Duncan started telling us about another high-end yacht that needed repairs. I had to admit, though, I was paying more attention to him than what he was saying. Up close, he appeared much taller than I'd remembered and had an easy smile. His eyes were a silvery-gray color, and every time he glanced my way, I felt jittery inside.

"I just realized something," Duncan said. "You're twins, aren't you?"

"Finally, someone with some sense," Nathan replied.

Duncan looked confused.

"Long story." Nathan slid his arm around my shoulders. "Yes, we are twins. She was blessed with the brains. Incredibly enough, I ended up with the looks. I guess you can't have everything."

I snorted.

Duncan shook his head and stared at us in amusement. "Sorry, dude, but I think you might have that wrong. Nikki here seems to have absorbed all the beauty genes, leaving you with a great sense of humor, though."

I laughed, secretly thrilled that Duncan thought I was cute.

Nathan pouted. "And I thought you invited me along because I was the cuter twin."

"No, but I have to say, you still have a nice butt," joked Duncan.

"Pilates," said Nathan, turning around. He flexed his butt-cheeks. "See? I could crack walnuts with this ass if I wanted to."

"How long did it take you to train for that?" Duncan asked, chuckling.

"Not too long. A few weeks. It's all in how you clench."

"Okay, enough!" I interrupted, still smiling. "Now I've realized that you are *both* a couple of dorks."

"From one dork to another," said Nathan. "I'm ready to see some yachts. I'll let you go first so you can concentrate on where to take us and not get distracted by my gluteus maximus."

"I think we're both distracted by the fact that you *are* an ass," I said dryly.

Duncan burst out laughing and turned around to lead us toward the marina. I quickly checked out *his* ass and decided that he definitely didn't need any Pilates.

9

AN HOUR LATER, after getting a few secret tours on some very large and luxurious yachts, we followed Duncan into the main shop to meet his dad, Sonny.

"Hello," Sonny said when we walked in. He was an older version of Duncan, minus the hair. "It's nice to meet the both of you."

Nathan held out his hand and shook Sonny's. "Thanks for letting Duncan give us a glimpse of some of these sweet yachts. You must be extremely busy with all of those boats out there."

"Tell me about it," the man replied. "I can barely keep up. I'm going to have to hire someone to help around the shop, especially now that fall is just around the corner. Many of these boats need to be winterized—and soon."

I looked at Nathan, who was already way ahead of me.

"What kind of experience do you need? I'm looking for a job," Nathan replied.

Sonny rubbed his bald head. "I can't imagine you'd know how to repair boat engines at your age, although Duncan does, but that's because he's been around them most his life. You know, I could still use someone to take care of the customers, order parts, and do some of the lighter maintenance. That would free up a lot of time for me and my son."

I could see Nathan was getting really excited. "Listen," he said, his eyes sparkling. "I'm your man. I'm a very hard worker and learn quickly."

Sonny leaned back in his squeaky chair. "Okay. We'll have you fill out an application and I'll certainly consider you. I do have a couple of mechanics who work the graveyard shift. What I could really use is someone who doesn't mind doing a little grunt work."

Nathan smiled. "Grunt is my middle name."

Sonny grinned back. "That's what I like to hear."

While Nathan started filling out the application, Duncan asked me if I wanted anything to drink.

"Um, sure... water?"

"Come on, I'll show you our luxurious breakroom."

I followed Duncan to the back of the shop and we entered into a small room. It contained a soda and snack machine, along with an old, rusty refrigerator that had seen better days.

He opened it up and handed me a bottle of water. "I'll give you one from my secret stash. If I don't hide them, they seem to disappear overnight."

I laughed. "Really? Thanks."

"So," he said as he sat down and stretched out his legs. "How do you like Shore Lake so far?"

"Honestly, it's kind of a hard question to answer. Last night we found a body near the lake, and today, one of the waitresses at Ruth's passed me a note that warned us to stay inside after dark and not invite any strangers inside."

His eyes widened in shock. "Seriously? Are you kidding me?"

I took a sip of the water and shook my head. "No, I wish I was." I set the bottle down and pulled out the note Amy had given me.

He read it and frowned. "Very strange. So, do the cops know whose body you found?"

"Some girl around my age. Tina Johnson?"

He scratched his head. "Tina Johnson? To tell you the truth, I don't really know many of the locals. I only stay with my dad during the summer and then for the rest of the year, I live with my mom in Minnesota."

I felt a wave of disappointment. "Oh, does that mean you're going back to Minnesota next month when school starts?"

He smiled. "I graduated last spring, so now I can stay wherever I want."

"What are you going to do now?"

Duncan sighed. "I don't know. I was thinking that I'd probably help my dad out while I take some engineering classes at the local college."

"What about your mom? Do you think she'll be upset?"

"I don't think so. She just remarried and is pretty busy with her new husband. My dad doesn't really have anyone else but me, so I'm probably sticking around here."

I took another sip of water. "Well, it sounds like your dad really needs you in more ways than one."

He nodded. "What about your old man?" he asked and then looked embarrassed. "I'm sorry, I probably shouldn't have asked. If he's passed away or something, I apologize for my lack of tact."

I smiled grimly. "Actually, there are times that I wish he *had* passed away."

He looked surprised.

"Sorry. I know that sounds really cold, but he's an asshole. Thank God my mom is no longer with him."

"Then cheers to that," he said, tapping my water bottle with his.

"Cheers."

He re-capped his water. "So, back to the dead girl. Do they think she was murdered?"

"No, it sounds like she liked to party a little too much and may have accidently killed herself."

"What about the waitress at the diner?" he asked, chewing on his lower lip. "That was pretty weird."

"Yeah. Nathan keeps telling me not to worry about it, but... how can I not?" I sat back in the chair. "Have you heard anything about missing people or other bodies being discovered near the lake?"

He shook his head. "No, not really; although, there have been plenty of people moving away recently. That's why I mentioned the cabins. Either people are selling or just renting out their lake homes."

"Hey, Nikki," said Nathan as he stepped into the breakroom. "Are you ready to get going? I want to pick up those steaks for Mom before it gets too late."

I looked at my phone and noticed it was already after seven. "Yeah, we'd better leave."

Duncan stood up. "Thanks for stopping by, guys." He lowered his voice. "By the way, I'll work on my dad so he hires you."

Nathan laughed. "Sounds good. You want to hang out some time? You can show me all the hot spots. Maybe we'll even let Nikki tag along."

Duncan smiled. "Yeah. That sounds great."

"Cool. Thanks again for helping me with your dad. I'll give you a call."

"Okay." Duncan looked at me. "Nice seeing you again, Nikki."

"You, too."

After we left the boat shop, Nathan asked if I was interested in Duncan.

"Just as a friend."

"You know we're twins. I can tell when you're lying."

"I'm not."

"Yeah you are. Either to me or yourself."

"Whatever."

He pulled out his keys. "I hope I get that job. Sonny seems pretty chill."

"I bet you have a great chance with Duncan pulling for you."

"Pulling for both of us." He gave me a knowing look. "I know why he wants me working there. So he can see more of you."

I snorted. "Right."

"He likes you."

I didn't say anything.

"You're trying not to smile but I can see it in your eyes."

"I don't know what you're talking about," I replied, trying to keep a straight face.

He elbowed me playfully. "It's okay. You just keep pretending."

"Whatever you say."

10

IT WAS DARK by the time we made it home. We found Mom on the deck, desperately trying to figure out the grill.

"Step aside before you blow us all up," ordered Nathan, handing her the package of steaks.

"No arguments here," she answered. "I prefer cooking on the stove myself, but the steaks taste so much better on the grill. Thanks for picking them up, by the way."

"No problem. Just don't give the sheriff mine, it's the thirty-ouncer," he replied.

Mom snorted. "I'm sure you'd have my head, you bottomless pit. By the way, we're also having potatoes, pasta salad, and corn on the cob. So pace yourself tonight, if you can."

He snorted. "That's it? No dessert?"

"I took the cheesecake out of the freezer. The one I bought yesterday. But… let's make sure our guest gets a piece before you get your mitts on it."

"Only one cheesecake? Are you sure that'll be enough?" he replied.

She stared at him hard. "It will be, as long as you wait until everyone else has had a piece before you devour the rest."

He smiled sheepishly. "Okay, I guess I can live with that."

She gave me a *can you believe that guy?* kind of look.

Used to it, I just grinned. "You look nice." She wore a lilac colored blouse and a new white skirt I'd never seen before. "Is that new?"
She smiled and smoothed out her skirt. "Thanks. Yes. I bought the outfit awhile back and forgot about it. By the way, how was your trip into town?"
"It actually started out a little strange," I answered.
"What do you mean?"
Nathan cut in. "Oh, she applied for a job at the local diner and some waitress slipped her a note with a creepy, ominous warning."
Mom looked alarmed. "What?"
I showed her the piece of paper and she frowned. "That *is* pretty odd. Maybe she knew the deceased girl? Who knows, she may think there was foul play involved."
"That's what I said. Maybe there was," I replied.
She handed me back the note. "The sheriff didn't seem to think so. We'll ask him about it again when he gets here."
"Okay." I put the note away. I wasn't going to hold my breath about him telling us anything further about the case. Having a father for a cop taught me that they weren't keen on divulging information like that.
Mom slapped at a mosquito. "So, did you guys make it to Duncan's boat shop?"
"Yeah. And his dad is hiring for shop help, so I filled out an application," Nathan replied, smiling.
Her eyes widened. "Wow, that means both of you might already have jobs before the end of the summer? That's amazing!"
"I hope so. I need money and a car, badly," I said.
"If you get a job, I'll see if I can somehow help you finance a vehicle. You can pay me back in installments. But, don't expect anything fancy," she said.

I grinned. "Seriously? Thanks, Mom." Excited, I threw my arms around her.

"You bet. I know it's tough not having a car; especially now that you'll be a senior," she replied, squeezing me back.

"And I'm sure Nathan's tired of driving me everywhere," I added.

He shrugged. "It's fine right now. Once school starts, however, things might change."

As I pulled away from her, my eyes caught a movement in the woods. I thought it might be a deer or some other wild animal, but then it shot up into the trees. Because the thing moved so quickly, I couldn't exactly make out what it was. But one thing I did notice, were two glowing red eyes.

I gasped.

"What's wrong?" she asked.

My eyes scoured the trees. "Something's in the woods. Its eyes were glowing, too. Just like the thing from last night.""

She looked alarmed. "What?"

"We should all go inside. It's dangerous out here."

"Oh, for God's sake." Nathan stepped off the deck and began walking slowly toward the woods.

"What the hell are you doing?" barked mom.

He raised his hand. "Calm down. It's probably just a deer or something."

"Really? Well," I pointed up toward the top of the trees, "it flew all the way up there, and I doubt it was one of Santa's reindeer."

My mom released a heavy sigh. "Then it was just a bird. Don't scare me like that."

I shook my head, vehemently. "No, it definitely wasn't a bird."

Nathan walked back onto the deck. "Of course it was. Or maybe a flying squirrel."

I put my hands on my hips. "It wasn't a small animal, okay? It was big! Bigger than you," I told him.

"The shadow probably looked a lot larger than the animal itself. When it's dark like this, your eyes play tricks on you. Think about it, nothing my size would be able to fly up into a tree," he said. "It's not possible."

"I know what I saw, and it was big. You guys can stay out here if you want, but I'm going into the cabin." I looked up again and shivered. "This place really gives me the creeps. Especially at night."

"It's been a long day for everyone," admitted Mom as I opened the patio door. "I know it's late and you shouldn't have to wait until nine to eat. If you're hungry, Nikki, eat some of that pasta salad I made."

"Okay." I looked at my brother. "Nathan, keep an eye out. Just in case."

"Yeah. Of course."

Frustrated that they weren't taking me seriously, I went inside and made my way into the kitchen. I opened up the refrigerator and took out the large bowl of pasta.

"That 'bird' would have to be the size of a damn ostrich," I muttered, irritated. I set the bowl onto the counter loudly and grabbed a large spoon from one of the drawers. As I began scooping out some of the salad, the hair on the back of my neck stood on end. I felt like I was being watched. Trying to remain calm, I slowly raised my eyes to the window in front of me. A pale face, with blood-red eyes, stared back at me through the glass. Leaping away from the window in terror, I let out a bloodcurdling scream and it disappeared.

My brother raced inside of the house. "What's wrong?"

I pointed toward the window. "Someone was watching me!"

He grabbed a butcher knife from the block and peeked outside just as Mom showed up.

"Is she okay?" Her eyes grew wide as she noticed the knife. "Nathan, what are you planning on doing with that?"

"Nikki thinks there's someone out there." He headed toward the sliding glass door. "If there *is* someone, I'm not going unarmed."

"We were just out there. We didn't see anyone," she replied.

"So, you don't believe me?" I asked angrily. "Again."

She sighed. "I'm not saying that."

The doorbell rang, startling us all.

"I'll get it," said mom, looking frazzled. "Hopefully it's the sheriff and he can take a look around outside. Put the knife away before someone gets hurt."

"Screw that. We don't know who's at the door. I'll get it."

"Fine," she replied.

We followed Nathan to the front door and he swung it open.

"Hello." said Caleb, smiling and holding out two bottles of wine. "I wasn't sure if you were a wine drinker or not. I brought a red and a white, just in case." His eyes took in the knife Nathan was holding. "Whoa, what's going on?"

"Thank God you're here," Mom said, grabbing the bottle of red wine and pulling him through the door. "Nikki thinks someone is lurking around outside."

"Think?" I snapped. "I *know* there is. Someone was in the woods watching all of us, and then a face stared at me through the window."

Caleb was dressed in civilian clothing, jeans and a white polo shirt, but he reached down by his ankle and pulled out a gun. "Okay, I'll go take a look. You guys stay inside and lock your doors."

"I know you guys think I'm overreacting, but I'm telling you that someone is stalking us," I said, as she locked the door behind him. "And you two have to start taking me seriously."

"I do." She walked over and hugged me. "Hopefully Caleb will find out who's doing it. I'm so glad he came early."

I was actually glad to see him, too.

"Hey. What if it's dad?" Nathan suggested. "What if he's found us and is trying to freak everyone out?"

Mom's eyes widened. She looked troubled. "Oh, hell, I never even considered that. Let's hope not."

I frowned. "I know he's mad at you but why would he be trying to terrorize all of us now? I mean, would he do that?"

She shrugged. "I don't know. I wouldn't think he'd try to frighten you and Nathan. But, who knows?"

"You didn't think he'd do what he did to you either," Nathan said grimly.

Mom nodded. "True. I can't imagine how he would find out where we're staying, though. The only person who knows is Ernie."

Nathan and I looked at each other.

"I think you should call Ernie and make sure he's okay," Nathan said.

She moved toward the phone, her face white. "Good idea. I'll call him right now."

There was a loud knock at the door. "It's me. Let me in. Everything's okay," called Caleb.

Mom put down the phone and rushed to the door. "Did you find anything?" she asked, when he stepped inside.

He smiled. "Actually, I found a couple of raccoons outside that were looking pretty mischievous. I didn't find anything else out of the ordinary, though."

Nathan went into his C.S.I. mode. "Did you see footprints by any of the kitchen windows, or any smudges on the glass? Maybe you could lift some prints?"

He bit back a smile. "I didn't see much, I'm sorry. But I really don't think there's anyone out there."

"I know what I saw, and it was definitely not an animal's face staring at me through the kitchen window. It freaked the hell out of me."

"Maybe it was an alien?" Nathan asked.

"Very funny."

"I'm being serious," he replied. "I mean, you never know. They could be thinking of abducting one of us. For experiments."

I'd never thought of that. The thought of an alien sticking tubes up different orifices in my body was horrifying.

Sheriff Caleb bit back a smile. "Let's hope not." He turned to me. "So, what did this 'person' look like?"

I sighed. "It was hard to tell, it happened so fast. I just remember they had a really pale face."

"Sure it wasn't green?" Nathan asked and smiled. "Again, I'm not mocking you or anything."

"I guess it could have been pale green," I replied. "It moved so fast. I only got a quick glimpse."

"It's still quite possible that you saw an animal and nothing more," Caleb said, walking toward the living room window. He lifted one of the blinds and peered outside. "Who knows, maybe it really was one of the raccoons?"

"It wasn't a raccoon. I'm sure of that," I said firmly, irritated that he, too, wasn't taking any of this seriously.

He released the blind and walked back over to us. "Sorry. I don't mean to upset you. I can see that you're really worried. If you want, I can look around again, if it makes you feel better."

Mom folded her arms and nodded. "Thank you, Caleb. We'd appreciate it. This family has been through so much that it would really be comforting if you could do that for us."

He smiled and nodded. "No problem, I understand. I'll be back in a few minutes."

"Thank you," I replied.

He headed toward the doorway. "No problem. I just want all of you to feel safe here. I'll be back."

"I told you he was a nice man," Mom said after Caleb left the cabin again.

Even I had to admit, it was almost comforting having him around. Almost.

Nathan looked out the window again. "I'm still going with the alien theory. This would be a prime location to find an alien baby momma."

"Stop." Mom looked amused. "That's disturbing."

"Hey, you never know. We're out in the middle of nowhere basically. Nikki is probably young and fertile. The perfect specimen," he replied.

I shivered. "Great. I'm never falling asleep again. Ever. Thanks, Nathan."

"You're the one who keeps seeing things. I'm just trying to help solve the mystery here."

"As much as I appreciate your theories, let's not panic. If it were an alien, I think we'd have heard or seen a spaceship," Mom replied.

"Not necessarily."

I listened as the two of them bantered back and forth. I still wasn't sure what was out there, but I wasn't feeling the alien theory.

11

THE SHERIFF TOOK much longer this time, but when he returned, he still hadn't discovered anything unusual.

"Thank you for doing that, Caleb," Mom said, handing him a glass of red wine. "You could probably use a little of this right now."

"I thought you'd never ask." He smiled and winked. "Although I'd better not overindulge; I hear the cops in this area are pretty terrifying."

She giggled and then turned to Nathan. "Honey, can you fire up the grill? I'm sure everyone is starving by now."

"Yeah, I'm literally fading away." Nathan raised his hands in front of his face. "I can barely see my hands."

"Be careful, Nathan," I warned.

"I'll be fine."

Mom smiled and shook her head. Then she turned to me. "Are you okay?"

I nodded and glanced at Caleb, who only had eyes for her at the moment. He was obviously hungry too, and for more than just food.

Gross.

"Why don't you go upstairs and rest for a little while. I'll fix you a plate of food and bring it up later, if you don't feel like coming back down." Mom smiled encouragingly at me.

"Okay, I need to change, anyway." I got up from the sofa.

"Yes. Get comfortable," she replied.

I raced upstairs to my bedroom, still feeling tense. The gnawing feeling of dread in the pit of my stomach was driving me crazy; I just wanted to go back to my old home in San Diego. I didn't care what anyone said, I knew what I saw. I also knew that we didn't belong here.

Feeling helpless, I kept the lights off and changed into a pair of shorts and a T-shirt, keeping my attention on the balcony door. Afterward, I grabbed the bat and slowly walked over to the glass and looked down below. I half expected to see an alien, or some kind of ghoul, l lurking around in the darkness. Nothing appeared out of the ordinary. However, it still wasn't enough to calm my nerves.

"What are you doing?" whispered Nathan next to my ear.

Startled, I gasped and glared at him. "N*ot* cool, Nathan! You almost gave me a fucking heart attack!"

He shrank back. "Sheesh. Sorry. You really need to try and relax."

Trembling, I rubbed the beads of sweat from my forehead. I really *was* a bundle of nerves. "I can't. Look, I don't care what the sheriff says, I saw someone out there watching me in the kitchen."

He sighed. "I'm not sure what you saw, either. What I do know is that ever since we found that girl's body, you've been going crazy. I mean, isn't it possible that you saw a raccoon staring at you in the window? You said so yourself, you couldn't even see the face very well."

"I can tell the difference between a raccoon's face and a person's, Nathan. I'm not a complete moron," I snapped, glancing through the window again. "And a raccoon is much shorter than a person. So, unless one was standing on another's shoulders, there's no way in hell *that's* what I saw."

"True. I never thought of that."

"Did you start the grill?"
"Yeah. Caleb's keeping an eye on it now."
"Good. I'd rather have him out there than you."
"Yeah."
We both stared outside in silence for a while.
"Maybe it really is Dad, then," he said dully. "He might be trying to freak us out."
"I don't know. It just doesn't feel right. Dad had major anger issues, but he doesn't seem the type of person who'd waste his time doing this kind of thing. In fact, he's probably hiding on the other side of the world by now with the help of some of his cop friends."
"Maybe," said Nathan.
I yawned. "I guess I'm going to bed. I lost my appetite, anyway. Could you let Mom know? I don't really want to go back down there. Watching them flirt with each other is annoying."
He chuckled. "Okay, Nik. If you need us, just holler."
I grunted. "Oh, you'll hear me. Count on that."
After he left, I turned on the television and watched a movie about a girl who'd fallen in love with both a vampire and a werewolf. I'd already seen it a million times, so my eyelids grew heavy fairly quickly. Ten minutes later I was out cold in my bed and dreaming of Duncan, who turned into a werewolf and was trying to kill my own vampire boyfriend. Every time I tried to see the vampire's face, however, it was blurred out; I couldn't make out any of his features. Just like the strange face in the window.

12

MOM WAS STILL sleeping when I woke the next morning. It was pretty odd, considering it was after ten and she never usually slept past eight.

"Hey," I said to Nathan, who was eating a monstrous bowl of cereal and watching television at the kitchen counter.

He smirked. "It lives."

"It also knows how to throw a right hook," I answered, shuffling past him.

Nathan laughed with his mouth full. "Hey, guess who called for you this morning?" he asked, when he was done chewing.

Duncan? "Who?"

"The manager at that diner you put in an application for."

I stared at him in surprise. "Wow, really?"

"Yeah, you're supposed to call her back if you're still interested in setting up an interview. Here." He reached over and handed me a slip of paper. "Call Rosie at that number."

"Awesome." Finally, some good news.

Ten minutes later I had an interview set up for later that afternoon. I told him about it.

Nathan nodded in approval. "Damn, that was fast. I guess I'll have to give you a ride."

I smiled. "Or, you could just loan me your car."

He snorted. "Right. Nobody drives that car but me. Not even Deanna got the privilege of driving my baby."

"Hi, guys," yawned mom as she stepped into the kitchen. She still had her pajamas on, and her hair was all askew.

"You were up late," said Nathan.

She turned on the Keurig and smiled. "Well, Caleb's an interesting man."

"Is that right?" Nathan replied, smirking.

"Yeah. He's traveled all over the world and we talked for hours about some of his crazy adventures."

Nathan chuckled. "Small town sheriff-slash-traveler extraordinaire, huh?"

She got this faraway look in her eyes. "He's been to so many places, it's amazing. It's kind of surprising that he ended up here, in this small town."

"Didn't he grow up in Shore Lake?" Nathan asked.

"No. He's only been here for a couple of years, I guess. Anyway, we had a lot of fun talking together," she replied, smiling to herself.

"Oh, shoot," I said. "Speaking of Caleb, I forgot to tell him about that note we received at the diner."

Mom waved her hand. "Oh, I mentioned it to him and he didn't seem too concerned. He'd heard Amy was having a hard time getting over the loss of Lisa. They were really good friends, I guess. It's made her a little… unstable."

"What did he mean by unstable?" Other than being worried, she seemed pretty sane to me.

She sighed. "I'm not supposed to talk about this, but the poor girl tried to commit suicide a couple of weeks ago."

"Wow," replied Nathan. "That's rough."

Mom nodded. "I guess her parents have been trying frantically to get her some help. She was even prescribed antidepressants. Obviously, she still has some emotional issues."

"And Caleb knew all about this?" It seemed a little strange that the family would tell the sheriff something so personal.

She poured some cream into her coffee. "Yeah, his daughter, Celeste, went to school with Amy. They're friends, apparently. That's how he found out."

"Oh," I said. That made sense. "Still, if Amy is having such a hard time, how is she able to work?"

Mom sighed. "She must be coping enough just to get by. It's sad."

"Yeah." My heart went out to her. I couldn't imagine what she was going through. It almost made me want to befriend her. To see if I could help in some way. I told them what I was feeling.

"It's noble that you want to do that. But... you can't save everyone, Nikki," she relied.

I frowned. "Mom, you of all people know that when someone needs help, they shouldn't be ignored."

Mom opened the refrigerator. "I'm not saying ignore her. I'm just suggesting that you don't have to take on someone else's problems when we have enough of our own."

I couldn't believe how insensitive she was sounding. It was odd, especially coming from someone who'd been through so much herself.

"I don't care. If I start working at the diner, I'm going to make myself available to her. To talk. Or, whatever. I mean, maybe she didn't just lose her friend, maybe it was her *only* friend."

"Perfect, Nik. You don't have any friends either," Nathan replied.

I gave him a dirty look.

"What? I'm just saying, you could both use a friend," he said defensively. "Hell, we could all use some, right? Even Mom has Caleb now."

"Exactly," I replied.

She nodded slowly. "Fine. Just, be careful. I know you want to help and that's sweet. It's just that we're trying to stay away from drama, and—"

"What the *heck*?" I replied. "Have you been listening to me at all?" *I just didn't get it.*

"Nikki. I'm just trying to protect you."

I snorted. "From a depressed girl? I don't need any protection."

She groaned. "Okay, okay, fine. Let's change the subject. How did you sleep last night?"

I shrugged. "Fine, although, I had some disturbing dreams. Other than that, I slept pretty well."

"No freaken way," interrupted Nathan. He turned up the volume on the television and a picture of Amy flashed across the screen.

My eyes widened in horror. "That's her, Mom!"

"The body of nineteen-year-old Amy Kreger was found in the woods near Lake Shore, early this morning," said the grim-faced female reporter, standing next to an old Chevy Camaro. "Her car was found abandoned by the side of the road with drug paraphernalia sitting openly on the front seat. When police officers were called to investigate, they found the deceased in the woods, her wrists slashed. Tragically, this young woman was close friends with Tina Johnson, who went missing a few weeks ago. Tina's body was found just two days ago, washed up onshore in an undisclosed location. Police officials do not suspect foul play in either case."

When they moved on to the next story, Nathan turned off the television and we all stared at each other

in shock. After the talk we'd just had, I felt like someone had just kicked me in the stomach.
Poor Amy.
As far as suicide went, I just wasn't buying it. My gut told me that if she'd wanted to kill herself, she'd have done it already. Not the day after she'd warned us about the dangers in Shore Lake. Someone had gotten to her.
I pointed at the television. "No foul play in *either* case? Right. This happened after she tried warning us."
"They reported it as being suicide," replied Mom, looking puzzled. "She was depressed, too. I don't know why you're thinking that this is anything but suicide."
"I'm with Mom on this one. Amy was distraught over losing her friend. Even the sheriff said she'd been having a hard time dealing with it. Not to mention that they found drugs in her car."
"Maybe it was planted," I replied.
"That would mean her death was carefully planned ahead of time. Why would anyone put that much effort into murdering a young girl and making it look like suicide? This isn't television," Mom said.
"Someone would if they thought she was a threat."
Mom sighed.
Frustrated, I stood up. How could they not see that things weren't adding up?
"We just can't go jumping to conclusions like this."
"Whatever, I'm going to lie down in my room for a while," I said, feeling dizzy. I still couldn't believe this was happening. *Was I really the only one in this house that thought this entire thing was sketchy?*
Neither of them replied.
Leaving the kitchen, I went upstairs and took out the note Amy had given me. It gave me the chills to know that she was now gone forever.
"Hey," Nathan said from my doorway. "I'm taking the boat out in an hour if you want to get some fresh air

and clear your head. I think it would be good for both of us."

I nodded. "Okay. Sounds good. Is Mom coming?"

He shook his head. "No, she's going into town to talk with her new boss. I guess she's starting work on Monday."

I groaned inwardly. Apparently, we really were staying in Shore Lake and there was no going back. "Okay. I'll be down in an hour."

Nathan left and I took a quick shower, still thinking about Amy and the face in the window last night. I wasn't sure at this point which was more disturbing. I knew one thing, however; I wasn't going to give up trying to talk Mom into leaving this town. Something was going on. Something sinister. I wasn't sure if it was just one crazy freak or a group of them. What I did know was that there were two dead girls and now someone appeared to be spying on us. At this point, even Dad seemed less frightening.

After I toweled off, I slipped on a pair of shorts and a tank top, then piled my hair on top of my head.

"Ready?" Nathan asked when I met him downstairs.

"Yeah, let me grab something to eat first." I hadn't eaten since the diner and my stomach was growling. "By the way, I thought Mom was going to save a steak for me?"

"You were asleep when she brought it upstairs. I didn't want it to go bad, so I ate it on your behalf."

I scowled. "It would have been fine in the refrigerator." It wasn't like we had steak much, so it was irritating.

"Maybe. I'll buy more when I get my first paycheck."

"You'd better."

"I will. Cross my heart and—"

"Don't even say 'hope to die'. There's been too much of that in this town already."

He grunted. "No, shit."

WHEN I ENTERED the kitchen, Mom was standing over the sink with the water running, her face pasty white.

I frowned. "Are you okay?"

She nodded. "Yeah, I think I had a little too much wine last night. It's finally catching up to me."

"Really? A delayed hangover? That's weird. What's that on your neck?" I asked, staring at her skin. "Looks like the mosquitos got you good last night."

She touched her neck. "Yeah. They must have."

The skin on her neck was definitely swollen and there were two small red bumps just below her ear.

I squinted. "Does it itch? It looks pretty inflamed."

She'd always been very sensitive to bug bites, so it wasn't a surprise that her neck looked the way it did.

She shrugged. "No, not really. It's pretty tender, though."

"You should put something on that," I said, turning away from her. I reached into the cupboard and grabbed a box of chewy granola bars. "Some of that Neosporin stuff."

"I will." She touched her head and groaned. "It's my head that's really bugging me. God, remind me not to have more than one glass of wine the next time anyone offers."

I snorted. "No doubt."

She grabbed a paper towel, poured cool water over it, and then dabbed her forehead. She sighed. "You know, I think I'm going to lie back down for a while."

"Hey," I said as she began walking away, "I forgot to tell you. I have an interview this afternoon. That diner I was telling you about." Amy's face flashed through my head, making me feel sad all over again. I still couldn't believe that she was gone.

Mom looked back at me and smiled. "Good job, sweetheart. I'm sure you'll get it."
Especially with Amy gone, I thought bitterly.

THIRTY MINUTES LATER, Nathan and I were racing across the lake in the boat again. With the fresh air and scenery, I started feeling a little better.
"Let's head over to Sonny and Duncan's marina!" he yelled over the engine.
I gave him the thumbs-up. I had to admit, the thought of seeing Duncan again was stirring up the butterflies in my stomach. I definitely needed something to distract me from thinking about Amy and the creepy things that had been happening.
The sun was hot, and by the time we reached the marina, my tan was beginning to deepen. Knowing that the rays were still damaging my skin, I grabbed the bottle of sunscreen and began applying it.
"Hey! Long time no see!" called Duncan, who was putting gasoline into a fishing boat.
"What's up, Dunc?" asked Nathan.
He smiled. "Not much."
Nathan docked the boat and tied it. "So, did your dad mention anything about the job yet?"
Duncan laughed. "Haven't had time to talk about it. But I think you have the best shot so far. He seems to like you."
Nathan looked relieved. "Cool. Nikki already has an interview later this afternoon for a waitressing job."
Duncan looked at me. "Ruth's?"
"Yeah. By the way, did you watch the news this morning?" I asked him.
He shook his head. "No time. I've been working."
I told him about Amy and then mentioned the face in the window.

His eyebrow shot up. "Seriously? Wow, it's weird that you mentioned that, because I'm pretty sure that someone was watching me last night, too."

13

MY STOMACH CLENCHED up like a tight fist. "Really?"

He nodded. "It was just before midnight and I was in the kitchen, having a snack. I heard some weird scraping noises near one of the windows, and when I looked up, I could have sworn someone ducked away. I even went outside to check it out."

I shivered. "Did you find anyone?"

"I didn't. But it felt like someone was watching me outside, too. I have to admit, it pretty much scared the shit out of me."

I turned to Nathan. "So, do you think I'm still seeing things?"

He looked at both of us and shook his head. "Fine, I believe you. Maybe it's a peeping Tom?"

Duncan shrugged. "Could be. It also happened to me a few weeks ago, too, but I thought I was just imagining things. In fact, now that I think about it, I believe it happened around the night that girl went missing, Tina Johnson."

I shivered. "And last night, Amy was murdered. Talk about a coincidence."

Nathan groaned. "Nikki, quit it already. You watched the news! They have evidence that she committed suicide. They found drugs in her car and her wrists were slashed. She was messed up. Caleb's daughter even told him she had issues."

"Maybe, but I still have a hard time believing there isn't more to the story. Someone could have killed her and covered it up. She was terrified of something. Why would she warn us if she wasn't?"

Nathan walked over and shook me playfully. "You're making something out of nothing. Okay, even if someone was watching both of you last night, it's probably just some pervert."

"And that's supposed to make me feel better?" I asked incredulously.

With a determined look on his face, Nathan said, "Fine. You know what? I think we should try and catch whoever's doing it."

"How?" I asked, my heart beginning to race. It sounded frightening and exciting at the same time.

Duncan spoke up. "I know. We could set up video cameras. I have some extra ones in storage that we keep for the marina. In fact, we could monitor both our cabins."

I nodded, feeling a surge of adrenaline flush through me. "Yes! If we can get something on camera, the sheriff will finally take us seriously."

"I think it's a great idea, too," replied Nathan. "If it's going to help you get over your paranoia, Nikki, I'll help Duncan set it up."

"It will."

"Okay," said Duncan. "I'm pretty busy this morning, but around lunchtime, I can get them out of storage and start setting things up."

"I have to bring Nikki to her interview this afternoon. We'll stop by your place afterward and you can follow us out to the cabin to set up something there."

Duncan nodded. "Sounds good."

"Thanks, Duncan," I said softly. "I've been going nuts about this."

Duncan's eyes met mine. "You're welcome. I'm just glad I can help."

"Me, too."

"We'd better get back," said Nathan, looking at his phone. "I'm hungry and Nikki probably wants to prepare for her interview."

Duncan's eyes lowered to my bathing suit and he grinned. "If she keeps that outfit on, she'll definitely get hired."

My cheeks burned red. I wasn't used to being flattered like that and it was thrilling, especially coming from him. I knew right then and there that I had a major crush on the guy.

Nathan snickered. "Wow, Duncan, I've never seen Nikki at a loss for words. Do you want to move in with us? Could sure use the peace."

Thank goodness for Nathan breaking the awkward silence. I flipped him the bird. "Very funny."

"Funny? I was serious." He untied the boat and pushed us away from the dock. "See you later, Dunc."

I smiled at Duncan. "Yeah, see ya."

"Goodbye and good luck with your interview, Nikki," he replied.

"Thanks."

As we drifted away and Nathan started the engine, I put my sunglasses on and watched as Duncan began fueling another boat. Not only was he cute, but he believed me, without question. So far, he was the only real good thing we'd encountered in Shore Lake. At least, for me.

14

THREE HOURS LATER, I sat across from Rosie, who'd inherited Ruth's diner from her mother several years back. As she looked over my job application, I studied the rail-thin, bleach-blonde, weather-faced woman and wondered how old she was. She seemed to have a lot of energy.

"You're new in town?" she asked in a gravelly voice.

"Yes, we just moved here a couple of days ago."

"Have you ever waitressed before?"

I sighed. "No. I worked at a boutique, though, so I've used a register before and have experience with customers."

She nodded. "You'll be on your feet a lot. Do you have any problems with that?"

I shook my head.

"Are you available to work nights?"

I bit the side of my lip. "I'd prefer days, if that's possible."

She studied me. "To be honest, I really need the help at night. I don't expect you to work past midnight, but my second shift is really hurting right now. I'm even willing to pay you an extra dollar an hour."

I thought about Amy's warning. It wasn't as if I'd be hanging around outside, though.

As if reading my mind, Rosie told me that one of the cooks could walk me out after my shift ended.

"Okay. Is there a chance I can switch to days in the future? When school starts, my mom won't want me working past ten."

She nodded. "We won't make you work past nine during the week, but we'd need you until midnight on Fridays or Saturdays. Would that be an issue for you?"

"No," I answered.

She asked me a few more questions and then hired me on the spot.

"Wow, that was fast," I blurted out.

She smiled. "We need the help, desperately. Can you start tomorrow?"

I nodded. "That shouldn't be a problem."

"You'll be training with Susan. So, we'll see you around four, tomorrow afternoon?"

I agreed and then she found me a uniform, which wasn't easy with my short frame. When it was all said and done, I left the diner with a smile on my face. I was so happy, I almost felt like dancing.

"Let me guess, they hated you," said Nathan as I got into his Mustang. He'd been listening to the stereo and waiting for me in the parking lot.

I snorted. "Not that much. I start tomorrow."

He high-fived me. "Good job. I also have awesome news; Sonny called me and I start next Monday. Pending a drug test. I'm sure Duncan had everything to do with me getting hired, but I'm not complaining."

"That's great!" I replied, but then swore. "So, how are we going to work this out? I need a ride to and from work until I'm able to get a car. They want me working second shift."

"If I'm at the marina, I'll try and work something out with Sonny. Maybe I can take my lunch break and pick you up at the cabin? I'm sure he'll be cool with that. It'll just be for a little while, anyway. Mom said she'd help you get a car."

I smiled. "Exactly. Thank you. I know it sucks having to drive me around everywhere."

"Yeah, you're kind of a pain in the ass," he replied, smirking.

I groaned and punched him in the shoulder. "You are an *ass* so I guess it kind of makes sense."

He rubbed his arm. "I must have a permanent bruise there from you beating up on me all the time. Show your brother some love once in a while, will you?" he pouted.

"Shut your yap and you won't get hurt."

"Ho, ho… big words from such a little twerp," he said.

I raised my fist again. "You don't listen very well, do you?"

He snorted and shook his head. "You're so violent."

I smiled. "And yet, you still love provoking me."

"The day I stop, you'd better start worrying. Speaking of violence, let's head over to the marina and check out the surveillance equipment," he said. "Maybe we'll actually catch your stalker."

I'd almost forgotten about it. "Okay."

Nathan gave me a sideways glance. "Although I'm sure Duncan will be monitoring someone else."

I pretended to act surprised. "What?"

Nathan smiled. "Oh, come on. You know he has the hots for you."

"Whatever," I said, looking out the window and trying to hide my smile.

"He does, but that's okay because he seems like a decent guy. I think you should go for it."

I snorted. "Go for it? Look, I'm not interested in going for anything right now."

"Right. That's why you blush every time he looks your way."

"I do not!" I lied. If I admitted the truth, he'd tease me even more.

"You're face turns as red as a tomato."

I could feel it burning right now as he teased me.

"See!" he laughed.

"It's just a sunburn!" I protested.

He shook his head and gave me a knowing look.

I turned up the radio and tried avoiding his smartass grin.

When we arrived at the marina, we walked to the cabin next door, where Duncan was adjusting his surveillance equipment.

"Hey, guys," he said, noticing us.

"Hi," I replied.

"Hey, bro. You all set?" asked Nathan.

He nodded. "Yeah, I've got cameras set up all around the perimeter of this place. There's no way I'll miss this guy if he comes back."

"You sure it's a dude? Maybe it's a chick watching you. Nikki, where were you around midnight?" Nathan teased.

I glared at him. "Ha, ha. Funny."

"Believe me. I'd know if it was Nikki and I wouldn't complaining," Duncan replied, winking at me.

Now that really made me look like a damn tomato.

Nathan saw me blushing and cracked up. Fortunately, he changed the subject. "You still want to do our cabin, too?"

Duncan nodded again. "Yeah, I'll follow you in my truck. I'm ready whenever you are."

Nathan snapped his fingers. "Shoot, I just remembered, I have to pick up mom's dry cleaning. Is it okay if Nikki rides with you and shows you where we live? You can start setting things up. I'll meet you both at the cabin as soon as I'm done."

My eyes narrowed. I didn't remember her requesting anything like that. In fact, she was supposed to drive into town herself sometime today. I didn't mention any of this, however. I didn't want Nathan admitting out loud that he was trying to get us alone together. Mr. Matchmaker.

"Sure." Duncan looked at me. "Should we get going?"

I nodded and then followed him to a white pickup truck that read "Sonny's Boat Repairs" on the side.

Duncan apologized. "Sorry, it's nothing fancy but it gets me places."

"Don't complain. It's much better than what I have, which is nothing."

Chuckling, he turned the radio on and glanced at me. "You look nice. How did your interview go?"

I grinned. "I got the job. In fact, I start tomorrow evening."

"See, I told you, you'd get it."

I looked down at my clothes. For the interview, I had worn a peach silk blouse and a mid-length black skirt with heels. Not used to wearing pumps, my feet were already killing me.

"I guess I know where I'll be eating dinner from now on."

I laughed. "It's *your* stomach. I'm not cooking, you know, I'm only serving."

He shrugged. "That's okay. I'll come in and be one of those annoying customers who sits and drinks coffee all day long, but I'll leave a much better tip."

"As long as you tip, I'll save you a booth."

"So," he said, changing the subject when the silence became a little awkward. "Do you remember anything about the face you saw in the window?"

Thinking back, I shook my head. "No, it left so quickly. I just remember that it was really pale. It definitely wasn't an animal like the sheriff suggested."

"You called the sheriff?"

"He came over for dinner. He has the hots for our mother," I explained.

He laughed. "Boy, he works fast."

I snorted. "No doubt. My mom is already looking at engagement rings."

He raised his eyebrows.

I grinned. "Not really, but the way she's been gushing about him, she may as well. Anyway, he went out and looked around for a while, but figured it was just a raccoon."

"And you don't believe it?"

"Hell no. I don't know of any raccoon tall enough to look through the kitchen window."

"What about Bigfoot?"

I smirked. "I didn't see any fur."

"Maybe he shaved that day?"

Obviously, Duncan was kidding. "So, you think some Sasquatch paid both of us a visit last night?"

Duncan smiled. "No. I'm just trying to put some humor into this. The truth is, I know there's nothing funny about what's happening. It's pretty creepy."

"Yeah. I agree."

I then explained about the feeling of being watched when we were on the deck and the shadow that flew into the trees. As I went on, he looked even more concerned.

"No shit? That's happened to me before, too. I thought I was imagining it and made excuses, thinking it was a large barn owl or something."

I could feel the goosebumps traveling up my arms again. This was getting more disturbing. I couldn't wait to tell Mom. She needed to hear that I wasn't the only person seeing things. "Whatever it was… stood as tall as you. I couldn't make out what it looked like, but it was something much larger than a bird."

"Hopefully, these cameras will pick something up. They have a range of one hundred feet. I'll make sure some of them are pointing toward the woods, too."

"Good idea."

When we made it back to the cabin, it was almost five o'clock and Mom wasn't around.

Duncan nodded in appreciation. "Wow, nice place."

"Yeah. It's gorgeous. Too bad I'm not enjoying it because I'm so freaked out at night."

"I don't blame you."

I showed him around the cabin and then we started unloading the truck.

I looked up toward my bedroom. "Is there a way you can put a camera near that balcony?"

"Have you seen someone looking through it?" he asked, incredulously.

"Actually, I thought I saw someone staring at me through the window in my bathroom when I was getting out of the tub."

His eyes grew round. "He actually saw you naked?"

I blushed. Was it a *he*? That thought made me even more embarrassed. "I think so."

Duncan smiled wickedly. "I guess it would be inappropriate for me to say, 'lucky man'?"

My jaw dropped and I smiled, unable to help myself. "Just a little."

He chuckled. "Sorry, that was uncalled for. A feeble attempt to flirt."

I looked at him shyly. "You were trying to flirt with me?"

His gray eyes burned into mine. "A little. Did it work?"

I didn't know what to say. One thing for certain— knowing that he'd been purposely flirting with me made me want to squeal with joy. Instead, I played it cool. "Well, I…"

Thankfully, Nathan pulled up in his car at that moment, disrupting our conversation.

Nathan got out of his vehicle. "Hey, guys."

"Hi," Duncan replied, walking past him. "Nikki just gave me a tour of the place, so let's start getting these things set up before it gets dark."

Nathan shoved his keys into his front pocket. "Sounds good."

"Where's the dry cleaning?" I whispered angrily when we were out of earshot.

Nathan gave me a shit-eating grin. "Oh, silly me. I must have forgotten it."

"You did that on purpose. Thanks," I muttered.

"You're welcome. It's the least I could do for my favorite sister. So"—he waggled his eyebrows—"did you shove your tongue down his throat yet?"

I pushed him forward, toward the house. "Ha, ha. Very funny."

15

IT TOOK A couple of hours to set up all the cameras. Mom showed up just as we were finishing up.

"What's all this?" she asked, looking bewildered.

Nathan explained that we were setting up surveillance to catch the peeping Tom.

Mom groaned. She was wearing dark sunglasses and looked like she was still suffering from her hangover. "I thought we were through with that?"

I cleared my throat. "Duncan had someone looking into his windows last night, too, Mom. It's not just us."

She raised her eyebrows. "Really?"

Duncan nodded. "Yeah and it was definitely not an animal."

Mom yawned and took off her sunglasses. There were bags under her eyes, and she looked exhausted. "Then I hope you catch whoever is doing it on camera and show the sheriff. It's probably just some pervert or something."

"Or a vicious killer," I added, surprised that she was acting so casual about all of this.

"Stop talking like that," she replied, pursing her lips. "Now you're beginning to freak me out."

"It's about time," I mumbled.

She frowned and then yawned again. "Listen, I'm going to lie down for a while. I'm so wiped out."

I was getting hungry and knew that meant Nathan had to be starving. "Do you want me to make you any dinner?"

She grimaced. "Actually, I've been nauseated all day. I'm going to eat a couple more crackers and then go right to bed."

"Duncan, would you like to eat at our place tonight?" Nathan asked as Mom trudged up the steps and into the cabin. "I make a mean frozen pizza."

Duncan laughed. "No, I wish I could. I have to head back before my old man starts hounding me again," he said, raising his cell phone. "He's already sent me a message, wondering where I am."

Nathan nodded. "Okay, thanks for setting all of this up. I kind of hope we see some action tonight."

"Here's my number." Duncan held out a business card.

He took it. "Nice."

Duncan grinned. "My dad made them for me to give to customers. Call me if something happens."

"Will do. Call me if you see anything." Nathan gave him his phone number and Duncan added it to his phone.

Duncan turned to me. "Good luck with your new job, Nikki. I'll give you a couple of days before I stop in and harass you."

I was already looking forward to it. "Thanks."

AFTER HE LEFT, Nathan and I walked around the perimeter of the house again to make sure all of the cameras were facing the right way.

He looked up toward my bedroom. "Glad we aimed one toward your balcony. We don't want some Romeo trying to steal you away at night."

"I still have Mom's bat. Anyone tries getting into my bedroom, I'll go ape-shit on them."

"I seriously doubt anyone can climb up there. Not without a ladder, at least."

I thought about the thing flying up in the trees. I wasn't so sure.

We went into the kitchen. Nathan made a pizza and then joined me on the couch to watch movies.

"So, what do you think of Mom dating Caleb?" I asked seriously.

He shrugged. "I don't know. He seems like a good guy."

"You don't think it's too soon for her?"

"Just like I said before—I think she's lonely and wants to feel protected. The town's sheriff sure fits that bill."

"I suppose. I'm just worried about her getting hurt."

"Nobody can hurt her as much as our old man did," said Nathan softly. "It's sad but true."

He definitely had a point.

I FELL ASLEEP halfway through some horror flick about zombies when several loud thuds from outside startled me awake.

I rose quickly. "What in the hell was that?"

Nathan stood up. I could tell he was as freaked out as I was. "I don't know."

Something heavy banged against the door, and we both jumped. It definitely wasn't a friendly knock.

"Shit, what do we do?" I whispered, trembling.

Nathan ran into the kitchen and came out carrying the butcher knife again.

I stared at him in horror. "You're not really going out there, are you?"

He swallowed and looked down at the knife. "I was considering it."

More loud bangs and I grabbed the phone. "I'm calling nine-one-one."

"Wait, it could be a raccoon or a bear."

I snorted. "A bear? Like you'd want to tackle that by yourself, anyway."

He swore. "I'm going to look through the window."

"Be careful." I followed him over. "Can you see anything?" I asked as he peeked through the gap in the blinds.

A look of alarm spread across his face. "Shit."

My eyes widened. "What?"

He turned toward me, his face as white as a ghost. "Check out the cameras."

I looked outside and gasped. Even in the dark I could tell that someone had destroyed all the surveillance equipment we'd set up.

"We need to tell Mom what's going on."

I nodded. "At least this time she'll believe us."

We raced upstairs and woke her up.

"What's going on?" she mumbled.

Nathan explained.

Startled, she called the police, and a half hour later, one of the deputy sheriffs arrived at the house.

"I don't know who did this, but they're gone now," he said, after checking out the property.

Mom let out a long, ragged sigh. "Why would somebody do this?"

"Oh, I don't know... so they wouldn't get caught spying on *us*?" I muttered sarcastically.

"Can you check for fingerprints or anything?" Nathan asked.

He nodded. "Yeah, I put a call in for a couple of our guys to get out here and do that, so try not to touch anything. They should be arriving any minute."

"So, where is the sheriff?" I asked.

The deputy pulled at the side of his moustache. "Caleb? Oh, it's his night off. He won't be back in until late tomorrow night."

Mom nodded. "He mentioned that he was going out of town today with his daughter."

"Celeste. Yeah. She's a looker," he replied with a gleam in his eyes and a weird smile.

Nathan and I looked at each other. It was an odd thing to say about the sheriff's daughter, even if it were true. I was willing to bet Caleb wouldn't be too happy to know that one of his deputies had the hots for her. Especially, this sweaty bald guy, who had to be somewhere in his fifties.

The cop, who appeared to be suddenly daydreaming, snapped out of it and smiled. "Sorry. Let me get a statement from you and then I'll be on my way. There isn't much we can do without any evidence right now. If we pick up something from the fingerprints, we'll proceed from there," said the officer.

"Sounds good," replied Mom.

After everyone was gone, mom dragged herself back to bed, but Nathan and I were still spooked and unable to sleep.

Nathan shook his head. "Duncan is going to be pissed when he finds out what happened. That was thousands of dollars in video equipment this person destroyed."

"Let's call him, it's only eleven. I'm sure he's awake."

A HALF HOUR later, Duncan pulled up in his white truck. Our eyes met immediately and I had to admit, I was really glad to see him. I felt much safer with both guys around.

"Wow," he said, as we examined everything. "This is crazy. I can't believe someone trashed all of these cameras. Did you see anything?'

"We heard the crashes but were too freaked out to investigate when it was happening," I admitted. "It actually happened pretty quickly."

"They must have even brought their own ladder to reach some of those heights," Nathan said. "Ours is locked away."

Duncan walked over to one of the trees and smiled proudly. "Sweet. They missed this one. I hid it pretty well. Let's go see if it recorded anything interesting."

Nathan put him in a friendly head-lock. "That's what I love about you, man. Always thinking."

"Let's just hope it captured something we can use," he replied.

FIFTEEN MINUTES LATER, we stared in awe at the video. Nothing we were seeing made any sense.

"What in the hell?" asked Nathan, moving closer to the screen.

We watched in disbelief as two of the other cameras were violently ripped from the house by something invisible.

"Ghosts?" I gasped incredulously. "I mean, are you seeing what I'm seeing? There's nobody there."

Duncan and Nathan looked at each other, both obviously stunned as well.

"This is freaking crazy. It doesn't make sense," Nathan said, looking rattled.

We rewound the video and watched it again with the same results. It seemed as if an invisible force had destroyed each of the cameras.

"Okay, common sense doesn't explain this at all," Duncan said, running a hand over the side of his face. "Maybe it's some kind of poltergeist?"

"If it is, we're definitely getting the hell out of here," I said firmly. The thought of the cabin being inhabited by ghosts freaked the crap out of me. I saw the movies Poltergeist and Amityville Horror. I knew when it was time to leave. Not after the ghosts tried killing you, but well before.

"We have to show the sheriff," said Nathan excitedly. "Maybe he can make some kind of sense of it."

I snorted. "Sense? A fucking ghost is messing with our minds, Nathan. You keep trying to make scientific excuses because you don't want to believe it. Look at the film. You heard the loud bangs. The cameras didn't just fall from the house by themselves. We've got to get the hell out of this house. Hell, this *town*." I looked at Duncan. "No offense."

"None taken."

Nathan sighed. "Okay. You're right. Something is happening that is beyond any logical explanation that we can come up with. We'll show Mom tomorrow, but we still need talk to the sheriff. If it is some kind of ghost, we'll get this place... exorcised or something."

"Maybe you should talk to the owners of the cabin?" suggested Duncan. "They might already be aware of these ghosts."

"Good point. That could be why we're renting it at such a steal," Nathan replied.

"What about your house, Duncan? How do you explain the face in the window or shadows flying into the trees?" I asked.

He smiled wryly. "Maybe the ghost is roaming the town? I don't know. None of this shit makes sense to me, either."

We watched the video one last time and then Duncan turned it off. "I'm going home to check on the cameras I've installed there, to see if they're still in place. I'll call you if I find anything else odd."

"Do you want us to come with you?" Nathan asked.

"No. My old man is home. I'll be fine," he replied, trying to look brave. I could tell by the look in his eyes, however, that Duncan was just as rattled as we were.

"Duncan," I said. "I'm sorry about the damaged equipment. I wish we could somehow replace it for you."

He waved his hand. "Hell, it's not your fault. If anything, we may have actual proof that ghosts inhabit Shore Lake," he winked. "We could all become rich and famous."

Or dead, like Tina and Amy.

"Hey, what if the ghost haunting us is Tina?" I suggested. "I watched this one documentary where a spirit attached itself to a family and followed them to other places. They couldn't get rid of it. What if the ghost followed us to you?"

Duncan's face turned a shade lighter.

"That's some crazy shit," Nathan said. "At least whatever it is hasn't come into our homes yet. I mean, that we know of."

We all looked around uneasily.

"Remember the note from Amy? Not to let anyone in at night?" I said in a low voice.

Nathan squeezed the bridge of his nose. "Okay, let's just get a grip here. We're making mountains out of molehills. I mean, who knows? Maybe someone tampered with the tapes?"

"Like who, Nathan?" I snapped. "And in such a short time? *Really?*"

He sighed. "Fine. This shit just freaks me out, okay?"

"It freaks all of us out," Duncan replied softly.

The grandfather clock struck the hour. We all jumped and then laughed nervously.

"Okay, it's late. I'm definitely leaving now," Duncan said.

We walked him out to his truck. As we watched Duncan drive away, I felt like we were being watched again. Nathan must have felt it too, because he looked toward the dark trees with an uneasy expression.

"We're definitely not in Kansas anymore," he muttered.

I agreed.

16

I WOKE UP around nine-thirty the next morning and noticed that Mom was still sleeping.

"She must be coming down with something," I said to Nathan, who I'd found outside sweeping up pieces of the broken video equipment.

He shrugged. "Could be the fresh air? It might be making her sleep better?"

"Maybe. So, did you hear anything from Duncan yet?"

"Yeah, he said his cameras were fine and there didn't appear to be anything unusual going on in any of the videos."

"That's good, I guess." I looked up toward my balcony. "I had a hard time sleeping last night. I felt like something was watching me again."

He laughed. "Probably me. I checked up on you a couple of times and you were snoring away."

I frowned. "I do not snore."

"How in the hell do you know?"

"Because you don't and we're twins," I answered.

He smirked. "I also pee standing up, does that mean you do, too?"

I snorted. "Whatever."

Nathan laughed. "I'm glad you didn't answer that. Anyway, as soon as Mom gets up, we'll show her the video and see what she thinks."

Just then, an old, red pickup drove up the path and parked next to Nathan's Mustang.

"I think that's our neighbor. What was her name? Abigail?" Nathan said, watching her curiously.

The older woman, possibly in her seventies or eighties, got out of the truck. Abigail was rail thin, with reddish-brown hair and watery green eyes. "Hello!"

Nathan and I greeted her back.

She smiled. "I just wanted to stop by and welcome you. Sorry it took me so long."

"No problem," said Nathan. "We should have come over and introduced ourselves."

"No worries," she replied, carrying a large pie pan over to us. "I hope you like strawberry rhubarb pie. I made it fresh, early this morning."

"We love it, thank you," said Nathan as she handed it to him. "Wow, it looks delicious."

"You're welcome. I grow the rhubarb myself. Anyway, my name is Abigail, by the way. I live at the next cabin over."

"I'm Nathan and that's Nikki," he replied, nodding toward me.

"Hi," I said, waving.

"Wonderful to meet you both. It's been quiet over here for so long. I was wondering when someone would be renting this beautiful place," she said, staring at it.

"It's amazing," agreed Nathan. "Every morning I keep pinching myself to see if I'm dreaming. We've never stayed in anything as nice as this before."

Abigail grinned. "It's probably the finest cabin in town."

"Have you ever met the owner?" I asked.

She shook her head. "No. Can't say that I have."

I thought that was a little strange, considering that Ernie had known about her husband dying recently.

"Have you lived here very long?" I asked her.

She nodded. "Yes. I grew up in Shore Lake. We get a lot of tourists, but the locals love it here and many never leave."

Thinking of the two locals who were recently found dead, I shivered.

"I'll be right back," said Nathan. "I'll put the pie in the kitchen. Can I get you a piece, Abigail?"

She shook her head and smiled. "No, but thank you. I made it for you folks."

"Okay, if you change your mind, let me know," he called, going into the house.

"So, it's just you two and your mother?" she asked. "I saw you three on the boat yesterday. It looked like you were having fun."

"We were. Our mother's not feeling well," I explained. "Otherwise she'd be out here greeting you, too. I'm sure she'll be sad that she missed you."

She smiled. "Oh, that's all right."

"I suppose you saw the police here a couple of times," I said.

Her smile fell. "Yes, I did notice that."

"We found a body the first night we arrived," I blurted out. "And last night, someone smashed our video equipment. We've been trying to catch the culprit. It's been pretty crazy."

"A body?" she said, her eyes widening. "Was it that young girl they mentioned on the news? Tina Johnson?"

I nodded. "Yes. They think she drowned and washed up here."

"They don't think it's… foul play?"

"Well," I said. "Personally, I think it is, but nobody else seems to believe it."

She stepped closer to me. "And why do you think it's foul play?"

I sighed. "Because we've had someone trying to scare us every night since we arrived. Then, the waitress who supposedly killed herself in the woods the other night, Amy? She gave me a warning the same day she died."

"What do you mean? What kind of a warning?"

"She slipped me a note at Ruth's, warning me not to go out at night and not to let any strangers into our home."

Abigail stared at me for a few seconds and then let out a long, ragged sigh. "Nikki, she gave you some good advice. If I were you, I'd stay in and not invite anyone into your cabin either. Especially those you don't know."

My heart began to pound. "So, you think it's dangerous out here at night, too?"

Her eyes hardened. "I know it is. My husband was killed by something evil." She glanced around anxiously as if someone might be listening. "Listen, there are things in Shore Lake that you don't know about; things you couldn't even imagine. In fact, I wanted to come over and warn you myself before I left town."

"You're leaving?" I asked, the hair standing up on the back of my neck. Hadn't she just said that the locals never left Shore Lake? This woman was scared to death, and after seeing the video from last night, I didn't blame her.

Just then, Nathan walked out. "Okay, I couldn't resist, Abigail, I had a little piece. And let me tell you, it was the best strawberry rhubarb pie I've ever tasted."

She smiled sadly. "Thank you."

Noticing her sudden melancholy, he asked, "Are you okay?"

Before she could answer, I said, "Nathan, Abigail was just telling me it's dangerous here at night and that her husband was murdered."

Nathan's stared at Abigail in horror. "Your husband was *murdered*? Do you know who did it?"

"Damn right I do. It was those vampires," she said without hesitation.

I bit back a laugh. Ghosts were one thing, but vampires? Even I couldn't accept something so ludicrous.

Nathan's eyes widened. "Excuse me?"

Abigail glanced toward the woods. "Shore Lake is infested with vampires. They could be out there right now. Watching us."

"Now, Abigail, everyone knows that vampires can't stand the sunlight," Nathan joked, winking at me.

"These aren't the kind you read about in story books. They're the real thing," she replied firmly.

"The real thing, huh?" Nathan said, still trying to hold back his laughter. "Well, thanks for the warning. I'd better stop by the grocery store later and pick up some garlic. These 'real' vampires hate garlic, don't they? Or is that another myth?"

"Don't mock me," she said, scowling at him. "I'm not joking, young man."

The porch door opened up and Mom stepped out. She wore dark sunglasses and still looked unusually pale.

"Hey. Perfect timing," said Nathan. "Mom, meet Abigail. Our neighbor."

She nodded and smiled. "Yes, I remember seeing you fishing the other day. Nice to meet you, Abigail. I'm Anne."

"Nice to meet you, too. Say, if you don't mind my asking, what's wrong with your neck?" the old woman asked.

The swelling on her neck appeared to be getting worse. She touched it and winced. "I don't know. I think

I was bitten by a couple of mosquitos, or maybe even a spider."

Abigail smiled. "I used to be a nurse. Can I take a look?"

"Sure," replied Mom.

She walked up onto the porch and examined the bites. After a few seconds she stepped back. "When did you get them?"

Mom shrugged. "I don't know, the other night when the sheriff was over for dinner. I didn't notice it until the next morning."

Abigail shrank back. "Sheriff Caleb?"

"Yes, the sheriff," I said, intrigued with her reaction. "Mom's dating him now."

"Is that right?" Trembling, Abigail backed away from her and then hurried down the porch. "I have to go. It was nice meeting you folks."

"What's wrong?" I asked. First her talk about vampires, and now she appeared to be spooked by the bites on my mom's neck. Then it hit me. "You're not thinking that the marks on Mom's neck are... vampire bites, are you?" I asked with a wry smile.

She opened her truck door and turned back to look at us. "I'm not thinking they are. I *know* they are."

17

MOM CHUCKLED WHILE staring at her in disbelief. "What?"

Abigail pointed toward her neck. "You've got the mark. If you don't get out of town while you still can, you'll be a threat to your children and everyone you love."

All of us watched her in stunned silence as she slammed the door and drove away, kicking up dust in her wake.

"Now *that* was really weird," I said.

"What a fruitcake." Mom turned around and headed back into the house. "Certifiable nutcase."

We followed her inside.

"She looked so normal. It just goes to show that crazy comes in many different forms," said Nathan. "It's a shame, too, because she makes a killer pie."

"We probably shouldn't eat it," Mom replied. "Who knows what she put inside of the pie."

I snorted. "Too late. Nathan already had a slice."

She looked at him and groaned. "Oh, Nathan."

"How was I supposed to know she was as fruitcake?" He shrugged. "Eh, don't worry about me. I have an iron stomach."

"If you start feeling ill, let me know right away," she replied, looking concerned.

His face paled. "Don't jinx me."

"I'm sure you'll be fine. Was it garlicky?" I asked, smirking.

"No. It was actually very, very good."

"Then I'm sure you'll be fine," she said, heading toward the kitchen. "She didn't think we were vampires until I walked outside."

Chuckling, I followed her. "So, are you feeling better today?" I asked, as she examined the pie.

"Actually," she removed her sunglasses and smiled wickedly, "I feel like turning into a vampire and sucking your blood. Blah!"

I snorted. "She was one weird old lady. Maybe she's the one trying to scare us?"

Her eyes widened. "You know, I never thought of that. I should mention it to Caleb when he comes over tonight."

"Are you guys going on a real date this time, or are *you* cooking, again?" I asked her.

"Actually, Caleb is planning on bringing me to his place. His daughter is making dinner for both of us, I guess."

"Mom," said Nathan, coming into the kitchen. "Did Nikki tell you yet?"

"Tell me what?"

He told her about the video and she followed us into the den to watch it.

"Something must be wrong with the camera," she said, frowning. "There's no way that video equipment fell to the ground on its own. Someone is playing games. I bet it's some of the local kids. Caleb mentioned that they can be mischievous."

"Mischievous?" I asked, frustrated. "These are not *kids*. It's an entity. A *malevolent* entity. Like a poltergeist."

"Nikki, I didn't even know you knew how to say the word 'malevolent'," joked Nathan.

I scowled at him. "You tell her, Nathan. She doesn't believe me."

Mom groaned. "First, all this talk about vampires, and now, you two with the ghosts?"

"Then how do you explain what happened on the film?" asked Nathan. "Even I'm having a little trouble with it."

She closed her eyes and rubbed her temples. "Seriously, I don't know. Maybe Duncan didn't fasten them down tight enough and they fell? Or maybe an animal pulled them down."

"I think we should show them to the sheriff and see what he thinks," said Nathan. "Because, you have to admit, this is some crazy shit."

"Nathan, watch your mouth." She sighed. "It's strange, I agree. Caleb will be here after nine o'clock to pick me up. I'll show him the video and see what he thinks."

"Thank you," I replied. Something told me that like Mom, however, Caleb would try to find a rational explanation for the footage.

"In the meantime," she said, shaking me playfully. "Let's not talk about ghosts, dead people, or vampires. It's driving me crazy! Okay?"

I nodded.

"You hungry, Mom?" asked Nathan, opening up the refrigerator. "I can make you something."

She smiled. "Could you? I'm starving. I'll go take a shower and you can make me whatever you want."

"Okay, how about a hamburger?" he asked.

She yawned. "Oh, now that sounds good."

"How do you want it prepared?"

Mom turned to him and smiled wickedly. "Bloody rare. I'm turning into a vampire, you know."

I SPENT MOST of the day watching television and thinking about Duncan. He planned on stopping by, after I finished work, and all three of us were going to try and record more ghost activity. Even Nathan now believed it was really a poltergeist and was talking about hiring an expert to help us.

"By then, Caleb will have seen the video," said Nathan. "He's got to believe that something is haunting us."

"Hopefully," I replied, not so sure.

Nathan dropped me off at the diner just before four o'clock. It was busy and the waitress who was supposed to train me, Susan, appeared stressed out.

"We're short-staffed and apparently, everyone in town wants to eat here today. Just follow me around for now and when it slows down, I'll go over the menus and tickets," she said, stepping around me with a tray full of food.

"Okay."

I followed her to a busy table while other customers tried getting her attention. She handed out the food and then I followed her back to the counter, where she handed me a coffeepot.

"Better idea, why don't you just go around and see if any of my tables need coffee or soda refills?" she said, pointing to her section.

Unfortunately, it never did slow down and I spent most of my time following her around or refilling beverages. At the end of the night, my feet were sore, but Susan had shared some of her tips, so I was happy.

"Sorry the training sucked today," she said, removing her apron. "We've been so busy ever since Amy…" Susan's face fell. "I'm sure you've heard by now."

I gave her a sympathetic smile. "Yes. I'm so sorry. Were you good friends?"

She nodded. "Yes, and she worked her tail off here. It's going to be hard to replace her, in many ways."

"I doubt that *I* could ever replace her," I said quickly. "In fact, she was the one who gave me the application in the first place. She seemed very nice."

She nodded and smiled sadly. "That's right. She mentioned something about that. Anyway, I'm sorry about today. If you can stay a little later tomorrow night, I'll go over everything else with you that we missed during our shift. Friday evenings are always busy, though, so plan on being here, late."

"Okay, thanks."

"Just remember two of the most important rules: the customer is always right, even when they're wrong, and to always smile, even when you want to slit their throats. Especially the super picky customers."

I chuckled. "Okay."

She stared at me for a minute. "Huh."

"What?" I asked.

"You know, you actually remind me a little bit of Amy. Different color hair, but your features are similar."

"Really?" I replied. "I guess I didn't seem to notice."

My cell phone began to vibrate.

"It's my ride," I told her and answered the phone.

"Hi," said Nathan, sounding irritated. "My damn car won't start."

My eyes widened. "What do you mean?"

He let out a frustrated sigh. "The battery must be dead or something. I'm trying to get ahold of Duncan, to see if he can give you a ride home."

"What about Mom's car?"

"I can't find her keys anywhere. Caleb's already picked her up, and she forgot her cell phone here on the counter."

"Great," I said dryly. "Okay, let me know if you talk to Duncan. I'll just hang out here for a while."

"Will do."

I hung up and Susan tapped me on the shoulder. "Sorry, I wasn't trying to listen in but… do you need a ride?"

I smiled weakly. "Actually, I might."

"My brother should be here in a half hour. I'm sure he'll give you one."

"Thank you. That would be great." I sighed. "I can't wait until I get my own car. Relying on someone else for a ride all the time is so frustrating."

"I know what you mean. I'm in the same boat. Anyway," she pulled out a pack of smokes from her purse, "I'm going outside to have a cigarette. Do you want to join me?"

"I don't smoke but I'll come out there with you"

We each filled a glass with soda, and I followed her out the back door of the diner to a picnic table. We sat down in the darkness across from each other and she pulled out a cigarette. "Thanks for coming out here with me." She grabbed her lighter. "I hate sitting alone out here in the dark."

"Why?" I asked, hoping Susan would open up. If she'd been friends with Amy, I knew there was a good chance that Susan knew what the girl had been frightened of.

Susan looked around. "It's a little… creepy."

The back of the diner consisted of a parking lot, where the employees usually parked, the lone picnic table, and a dumpster. Normally, I wouldn't have thought it to be 'creepy', just boring, but after the last few days, I could only agree with her.

Susan took a long drag of her smoke. "Oh, man, I needed that."

"So... you said you were friends with Amy," I said. "How long did you know each other?"

"For a long time. We went to school together," she said, her voice cracking. "I still can't believe she's gone."

"She seemed so nice," I replied, not knowing what else to say. I wasn't ready to come forward with the warning I'd received from Amy just yet.

Susan looked at me and nodded. "She *was* a sweetheart. Her boyfriend, though, he was scary. I'm glad she dumped him."

My eyes widened. It shouldn't have been a surprise. She'd been pretty enough. "Amy had a boyfriend?"

She blew out another stream of smoke. "Yeah, Ethan. He hangs out here sometimes at night with his crew. They're all kind of freaky if you ask me."

"Freaky? In what way?"

Susan shrugged. "I don't know, there's just something strange about them. They come in here, hardly saying a word to each other. They just sit and stare at us, sipping their coffee. Ethan is the scariest. He's cute, but there's something about him that makes me nervous. He has these penetrating blue eyes that give me the creeps. Anyway, I really hate serving them, but they're paying customers, so we can't exactly kick them out."

"Weird. So, why did she break up with this Ethan guy?"

She smirked. "Amy always had quite the imagination. Everyone thought she was a little... nuts, and maybe, she really was. I mean, she did kill herself. Anyway, she once told me she thought he was a vampire."

I choked on my diet soda. "What?"

"I know, right?" she chuckled. "A freakin' vampire, she said. Although, if I did believe in vampires, he'd be the first on my list of suspects."

Goosebumps raced up my arms and I shuddered. First Abigail, and now Amy—both believed there were vampires roaming the town. It sounded crazy and yet... I was starting to get the heebie-jeebies.

"We'd better go back inside," she said, putting out her cigarette. "My brother will be here soon. I'll see if he can give you a ride."

My cell phone went off again as we entered the diner. It was Nathan.

"Duncan's coming to pick you up."

"Great, thanks," I replied.

"Make sure he brings you straight home. No stopping at the local make-out point."

I rolled my eyes. "Ha-ha. You are such a comedian."

He laughed and hung up.

"I'm getting a ride from a friend," I told Susan afterward. "Thanks for the offer, though."

"No problem. Oh, my brother's in the parking lot," she said, looking at her phone. "He just texted me. I'll see you tomorrow, at four o'clock again?"

"Yeah. Have a good night."

"You, too."

After she left, I sat down at one of the booths to finish my soda and wait for Duncan. As I watched the front door, a group of kids around my age walked through. One of the two waitresses on duty seated them.

"Same as usual?" asked the older waitress, who I'd met earlier. Her name was Darlene and I knew she was close to retiring.

"Yes. Just coffee," broad-shouldered, dark-haired guy replied. Apparently, he was ordering for everyone. I watched as he handed her back the menu and our eyes met.

Embarrassed, I looked away quickly and stared outside at the parking lot, watching for Duncan.

Before I knew it, someone slid into my booth and I was suddenly facing the stranger who'd ordered the coffee. Our eyes met and I was struck with how stunningly good-looking he was. A level of gorgeous that was staggering. Dark, wavy hair, closely trimmed on the sides. Tiger-slanted icy blue eyes. High Cheekbones. Lips that were smiling at me in the most bewitching way.

At *me*.

My cheeks turned red. "Um, hi," I said shyly, wondering what this extremely hot guy wanted with me.

"Um, hi, yourself," he said with another slow, lazy grin.

We stared at each other and I couldn't seem to take my eyes off of him. "What's your name?" he asked softly.

I could barely get it out. "Nikki."

"I'm Ethan." His lip twitched. "But you already knew that, didn't you?"

I nodded.

I'd suspected he was Amy's ex the moment he'd stepped into the diner with his friends. There was definitely something different about him. Something that both frightened and fascinated me.

As if reading my mind, his smile deepened. "You're new in town?"

"Yes," I replied.

"Welcome to Shore Lake," he replied, his eyes burning into mine.

"Thank you."

My stomach began to grow warm and fluttery. The sensation traveled down to my pelvis, making me tingly and in need of something that I couldn't quite put my finger on.

He glanced toward the parking lot. "You must be waiting for someone. Who?"

"A friend," I said breathlessly. My heart pounded in my chest and I felt a strong urge to touch him. The impulse was so unnatural for me. I didn't exactly know what to make of it.

What if he really was what Amy had claimed him to be?

Common sense told me that there were no such things as vampires, but still... I sensed something not quite right about Ethan. Or me at that moment.

"Are you okay?" he whispered, reaching his hand toward mine.

I stared down at it, wondering what it would feel like to have him touch me. Would his skin be cool?

"Nikki," interrupted Duncan, snapping me out of it. He stood next to our table and looking pissed. "Are you ready to go?"

A wave of relief swept through me. "Yeah," I said. "I'm ready."

"Goodbye, Nikki," Ethan said, staring up at me as I got out of the booth. His eyes twinkled. "I'm sure we'll meet again."

"Goodbye." I looked away quickly. I was still confused at the intense rush of desire, and for a total stranger. How did that even happen?

"Who was that?" Duncan asked in the parking lot.

I could feel Ethan's gaze on me as we headed toward the truck. I wanted to look back but was too scared. "You might think I'm crazy, but I think that guy was a vampire."

18

"SAY WHAT?"

"WAIT until we get into the truck."

"Okay."

Once we were safely inside, I locked my door and looked at him. "Amy was convinced that her ex, that guy in the diner, was a vampire, and there's something about him that... scares me."

He shook his head and smiled as he started up the truck. "Okay. I'm on board with a ghost haunting your cabin, but a vampire in the local diner? How am I supposed to respond to that?"

I sighed. "I know it sounds crazy. It's just that there's something so strange about him. He made me feel..."

His eyebrows knitted together. "He made you feel *what*?"

Bewitched.

Horny.

I swallowed hard. "Weird, I guess?"

I wasn't about to tell Duncan that at one moment, I wanted to jump Ethan's bones and probably would have, if we'd been alone. It didn't even make sense to me. I'd hardly even kissed a guy...

Duncan looked back toward the diner. "Weird, huh? Well, if he gives you any problems, let me know."

"Okay."

We pulled out of the parking lot in silence as I thought about the strange encounter. Duncan glanced at me a couple of times, and I could tell there was something on his mind as well.

"What's wrong?" I asked him.

Not saying anything, he pulled over to the side of the road.

"What is it, Duncan?"

He tapped the steering wheel a couple of times and then looked at me. There was a grim smile on his face. "When I approached you with Ethan, you almost looked like you were ready to tear his clothes off or something. I don't know; it just made me feel a little... jealous."

"Really?"

He nodded. "The thought of another guy touching you... I don't know."

"*You* haven't even touched me," I murmured.

Duncan let out a ragged sigh. "Believe me, I've wanted to."

I wasn't even sure how it happened, but the next thing I knew, I was straddling him in the front seat and our tongues were down each other's throats.

"Nikki," he groaned against my lips.

My heart pounded madly in my chest as we explored each other's mouth. My entire body felt like it was on fire and I could feel his excitement as well. I ran my fingers through his hair and rocked against him.

Groaning, he pulled away and looked into my eyes. "I don't think..."

"Don't think," I replied breathlessly, pulling him back toward my lips. There was an intense hunger inside of me, one that I'd never felt before. I wanted to tear away both of our clothing, just so I could feel our skin moving against each other.

His mouth was hot, and soon he was kissing my neck while his hands moved under my shirt. As he was about to slide his fingers under my bra, my cell phone rang, startling us both. He quickly removed his hands and I got off his lap.

My face was burning with embarrassment as I fumbled for my phone. "Yeah?" I said into it, unable to look at Duncan.

"Hello to you, too," said Nathan.

I cleared my throat. "Sorry."

"You guys almost home, yet?"

"Almost," I lied.

"Good, I ordered a pizza and it's already here, so hurry the hell up."

"Okay." I hung up and stole a glance at Duncan.

"I'm sorry," he said, looking bewildered. "I don't know what came over me."

I stared at him in disbelief. "What came over *you?* I practically raped you." I suddenly felt foolish and hoped he didn't think I was a slut. "I've never done that before, to anyone. I'm sorry."

His lips curled up. "It's okay. At least I know you like me."

I laughed. "Good observation."

"I'm sure you could probably tell that I liked you, too," he said, grinning.

I thought about the way I'd gyrated on his lap and my cheeks grew hot. I changed the subject. "So, I hope you're hungry. Nathan has a pizza waiting for us."

"Oh, I'm starving, all right," he said under his breath.

I couldn't read his expression.

Was he angry with me?

I hoped to hell he didn't think I was a blue-balling bitch. I still couldn't get over the way I'd attacked him.

"Duncan, I don't know what to say. I mean I don't regret what just happened, but I feel like it was too fast. And that was my fault."

He gave me a reassuring smile. "It's okay. I'm not in a rush for anything. Don't go blaming yourself either. We both got caught up in the moment."

I relaxed. "Thank you. I really do like you, you know. I'm just..."

He touched my knee gently. "You have nothing to explain. It's okay."

It wasn't okay. I really liked Duncan but had never felt such a hot, carnal desire for anyone before. What was even more unsettling was that it had started in the diner. With Ethan.

Had he ignited it?

Even now as I thought about him, I could feel a lustful stirring down below. Maybe Ethan really was a vampire and had given off some kind of weird pheromone?

Or maybe you're as crazy as Abigail and Amy...

I almost hoped that was the case. It had to be better than the alternative—real life monsters.

WE RODE IN silence the rest of the way to the cabin. When we arrived, Nathan was sitting on the porch, holding a BB gun.

"We come in peace," teased Duncan, raising his hands in the air.

Nathan grinned. "Sorry. I was beginning to freak myself out, so I grabbed my old BB gun. I thought I heard some noises in the woods. But then, I actually found a couple of raccoons prowling around. Go figure."

We both smiled.

Duncan looked toward the woods. "Is the video camera still set up?"

"Yeah. I think we should hang out on Nikki's balcony and watch from above. See if we can see anyone sneaking around," Nathan suggested. "Just in case it isn't a ghost, but some jackass trying to screw with us."

Duncan nodded. "Good idea."

We went inside, grabbed the box of pizza and some plates, and then headed up to my bedroom. On the balcony, Nathan had set up three chairs and a small card table. We sat down and started eating.

"Where did you find the table and chairs?" I asked him.

"In the cellar," he said.

"Oh, cool."

Nathan grabbed another piece of pizza. "There's a lot of interesting stuff in there. You should check it out."

"I'll take your word for it," I replied. Mom had told us that there might be mice in the cellar. I wasn't about to see if she was right.

"How was work?" Nathan asked.

"Busy. I met this girl named Susan who was friends with Amy."

Nathan grinned. "Is she cute?"

I grunted. "God, is that all you think about?"

"*Is* there anything else, Dunc?"

Duncan smiled but didn't say anything.

I steered the conversation back. "Anyway, Susan was telling me that Amy believed her ex-boyfriend, Ethan, was a vampire."

Nathan snorted. "Yeah, I'd say Amy was a little messed up."

"I don't know," I replied, staring at my pizza. "She might have been right."

He looked at me like I was crazy. "Excuse me?"

"I met Ethan tonight and there was something really strange about him," I explained.

Nathan smirked. "He was dating Amy at one point. That tells you enough right there."

"Seriously, Nathan. It was so strange. He came over and sat by me at the restaurant. When he looked into my eyes, I almost felt like… I wasn't totally in control."

"What is that supposed to mean?" asked Nathan.

"I can't explain it," I said, looking sideways at Duncan. There was no way I was going to explain my desire to jump Ethan's bones, especially after what had happened between us in the truck.

Nathan sat back and blew out a weary sigh. "There is no such thing as vampires, period. Quit letting Abigail's and Amy's crazy notions play with your mind. I mean, come on, Nikki, you know better than that."

I shrank down in my seat. "I know. It's just... I can't explain it. There's something not right about that guy."

Nathan looked at Duncan. "What do you think about all of this?"

Duncan shrugged. "I don't know. I think something strange is going on and I'm not ruling anything out."

Nathan snorted. "Even vampires?"

"Maybe this Ethan guy believes he's a vampire and knows how to manipulate other people into believing it, too," said Duncan.

Nathan sighed. "I guess that sounds a little more reasonable to me. Maybe he knows how to actually hypnotize people. That would explain how Nikki believed she was under some kind of spell."

"Maybe," I answered.

We ate the rest of the pizza in silence, watching the woods and keeping an eye out for unusual activity. It was pretty silent, except for the leaves rustling in the wind and the crickets chirping.

"Anyone want something to drink?" asked Nathan, standing up. "That pizza is damn salty."

"I'll take some water."

"Me, too," answered Duncan.

When Nathan left us alone, I stole a glance toward Duncan, who I found was already staring at me in the darkness.

"What?"

He smiled. "I was just thinking how beautiful you looked in the moonlight. I know that sounds like a line, but it's true."

I returned his smile. "Thanks, Duncan."

He clasped his fingers and rested his chin on them. "So, spill it. Did you leave a broken heart back in California?"

I snorted. "No. In fact, I guess you could say I haven't had many boyfriends."

"I find that hard to believe. The guys there must be blind and stupid."

I blushed. "It's not like I didn't get asked out. I just wasn't interested, I guess."

"So, would you be interested now?"

"It depends on who's asking," I said, smiling.

After what had happened between us, I didn't think he'd have to ask. Admittedly, I'd been determined not to get involved with any guys in Shore Lake. But, I also hadn't expected to meet Duncan. He was sweet, handsome, and didn't treat me like I was an over-imaginative girl. Not like my brother and mother usually did. They never took me seriously.

He smiled. "I think we both know who's asking."

"I think we both know the answer then," I flirted back, surprising myself.

"Duncan," Nathan said as he stepped back onto the balcony, holding our drinks. "I almost forgot, could you take a look at my Mustang? I think it's the battery I'm having problems with, but I want to make sure."

"Sure. Do you have a battery tester?"

Nathan scratched his chin. His eyes lit up suddenly. "Actually, there might be one in the garage, I never even thought about looking."

Duncan grabbed a napkin and wiped the grease from his hands. "Let's go and check it out."

"Sounds good." Nathan looked at me. "Nikki, you can keep watch from up here and let us know if you see anything."

"Okay."

"Here's the BB gun." He handed it to me. "You still know how to use it?"

The gun felt heavy in my hands, even though I'd held it plenty of times before. "Yeah. I doubt I'd be able to shoot anything with it, though."

"To be honest, a BB gun isn't going to do much anyway," Nathan said. "Unless you can shoot someone in the eye with it. If it's a poltergeist, however, there isn't a weapon on earth that will stop it."

"Good advice," I said dryly.

"You'll be fine," he replied, patting me on the shoulder.

Duncan gave me a reassuring smile. "Holler if you see anything."

"Oh, I will," I said, watching them step back into my bedroom.

Moments later, I heard the front door open and then Nathan's laughter echoing in the darkness below. I watched as the guys stepped away from the cabin and headed over to the oversized garage.

"Nothing to be afraid of," I murmured to myself, staring toward the dark woods.

Suddenly, an owl hooted and I felt a chill in my veins. It was a bad sign. At least in the movies.

My eyes darted quickly from one side of the yard to the other. My breath caught in my throat as I saw what looked like a shadow move across the grass. I looked up into the sky to see where it was coming from, but saw nothing out of the ordinary.

I let out a shaky breath. Obviously, my overactive imagination was playing tricks on me again.

"Nikki," a voice whispered behind me.

Alarmed, I whipped my head around but saw no one. Still, I didn't feel like I was completely alone.

Ethan?

"No, that's ridiculous," I said breathlessly, my heart pounding in my ears. "There are no such thing as vampires."

"Nikki..."

Frightened, I shot up out of the chair and moved away from the table. Hot breath brushed against the back of my neck. I whirled around again, this time seeing a blurry haze of movement.

"Oh, my God... Nathan!" I screamed, running into my bedroom. I ran downstairs and threw the front door open. "Nathan!" I yelled, again.

Nathan and Duncan rushed out of the garage toward me.

"What's wrong?" called Nathan.

I pointed up toward my bedroom. "Someone... was... on the balcony," I gasped, out of breath.

His eyes shot up. "Who?"

I shook my head. "I don't know. I heard my name and then I felt someone breathing against the back of my neck."

Nathan frowned. "But you didn't see anyone?"

"No, but I *heard* them," I said, noticing the doubt in his eyes.

"Okay." Nathan took the BB gun from my hands and then rushed past me toward the house.

"You want me to come with you?" called Duncan.

"No. Just watch my sister," he hollered back.

Duncan, seeing how shook up I was, put his arms around me. "Are you okay?"

I nodded and leaned into him, closing my eyes. I could still feel the warm breath on my skin. It had been real. And so had the voice. Nathan *had* to realize that I wasn't imagining it.

Suddenly, Duncan was ripped from my arms and thrown backwards.

"Duncan!" I screamed as he landed on the ground.

"What in the hell was that?" he answered with an incredulous look on his face. He got up and began walking back toward me.

There was a flash of movement and Duncan went flying through the air again, much farther this time.

I stared in horror. What in the hell?! "Oh, my God!"

"What's going on?" Nathan called down from my balcony.

Duncan got back up again. "Something is trying to separate us!"

Panicking, I rushed toward him but didn't make it too far. Something swooped me up into the air.

"Help!" I screamed in terror.

I could feel strong arms holding me, my back against his chest. We were moving like the wind, going so fast that my eyes watered. The next thing I knew I was lying in the grass and staring up into a pair of familiar blue eyes.

"I told you we'd meet again," whispered Ethan, trailing a cool finger down my cheek.

I was paralyzed with fear as his eyes burned into mine. A familiar yearning spread through my veins and my terror turned to lust. I felt hot and bothered, ready to surrender myself to anything and everything he demanded.

"Sweet Nikki," he whispered with another of his bewitching smiles. He lowered his lips to mine and began kissing me. At first softly, and then with an urgency that took my breath away. His mouth was hot, his tongue probing and demanding.

"Ethan," I moaned when he moved his lips to my neck and made a hot trail toward my collarbone. My entire body trembled with desire. "Oh, God."

He chuckled softly against my skin. "Not quite."

I stared up at the moon as his mouth moved across my skin. I was under his spell. I knew it and I didn't care. All I wanted was for him to continue what he was doing. It felt so good. So right. I arched against him, moaning in pleasure as his hands moved to my breasts.

"Nikki!" hollered Duncan.

I stiffened up, his voice bringing me back to reality. "Duncan?"

Ethan raised his head and I could see the red rage burning in his eyes. "Fool," he growled.

Duncan crashed through the bushes right as Ethan took off. "Are you okay?" he asked, panting and out of breath.

I took his hand and stood up. "I think so."

"What in the hell just happened!" hollered Nathan, stumbling through the woods with a perplexed expression.

My legs suddenly felt like jelly. I looked around, wondering where Ethan had taken off to. And how he'd gotten us there so quickly. "I really don't know."

19

NATHAN AND DUNCAN were full of questions as we walked back to the house. I was still in a state of confusion and had a difficult time answering them.

"Who was it?" asked Duncan. "Or better yet, *what* was it?"

For some reason, I couldn't get the words out.

"Where'd they run off to?" asked Nathan.

"I... have no idea," I answered.

My thoughts were muddled because of my overwhelming attraction toward Ethan. Part of me understood that it wasn't natural; it was some power he was using to control me. Another part of me didn't care. I wanted to feel what it was like being with him again. It was almost as if I was now an addict and he was my addiction.

Nathan scratched his head. "Did you see who it was, Duncan?"

He shook his head. "I was thrown backwards and then Nikki was gone in a flash. It was crazy."

Nathan scowled. "I don't even know how to call this one in to nine-one-one. Attempted kidnapping by the invisible man?"

I cleared my throat. "Don't worry about it, Nathan. I'm fine."

"No, we have to call the police. You could have been hurt badly," he said angrily.

"I didn't see anything. I don't even know who it was. The cops are going to think we're all crazy."

Nathan stared at me for a minute. "Was it even human?"

"To be honest, I don't know," I muttered.

"Whatever it was had a temper. I could feel the animosity when it separated us." Duncan grabbed my hand. "I'm calling my dad to let him know that I'm staying over tonight. I'm not letting you out of my sight again."

Nathan looked at both of us, a confused look on his face. "Wait a second, did I miss something?"

I smiled.

"I guess you could say that I'm kind of falling for your sister," said Duncan with a sheepish grin. "I hope you're okay with it."

Nathan snorted. "Of course I'm fine with it. Now I won't be the only guy who has to suffer her P.M.S."

I slugged him in the shoulder. "Very funny."

"See," he said, moving away from my fist, which was cocked again. "She's volatile. If you're lucky, you'll be able to go out into public without bruises on your arm."

"Heads-up, your mom's home," said Duncan, as we walked out of the woods.

I frowned at the scene before us. She's just gotten out of the sheriff's car and he was helping her walk toward the steps.

"Sheriff, what's wrong with her?" asked Nathan, as we approached.

Caleb smiled. "She enjoyed one too many glasses of wine again. I brought her home so she could sleep."

Mom gave us a lopsided grin. "Hi, my babies..."

I groaned. It was obvious that she was totally hammered.

"Nikki and Nathan, I love you both so much," she said, swaying after Caleb let her go.

Nathan and I put our arms around her and held her up. "Wow, Mom," I grunted, trying to hold her up. "I think it's time you started laying off the wine."

Her smile fell. "Wine? I didn't have anything to drink."

"Sure you did," interrupted the sheriff. "Don't you remember the Cabernet you picked out yourself from the wine cellar? We had it with dinner."

Mom looked confused but then when her eyes met Caleb's, she smiled wickedly. "All I remember is dessert."

"Okay, T.M.I.," I replied as Nathan and I swung her away from Caleb and into the house. The idea of her and Caleb getting it on was disturbing.

"I'll call you tomorrow night!" Caleb called out.

"Okay!" she replied.

Nathan looked at me. "Nikki, can you take care of Mom? I'm going to talk to the sheriff."

I nodded and then proceeded to help her upstairs, which wasn't an easy task. When we finally made it to her bedroom, she passed out the moment her head hit the pillow. I removed her shoes and covered her up with a sheet as she began to snore.

Duncan appeared just as I was closing her bedroom door. "Nikki, the sheriff wants to talk to you."

I nodded.

He grabbed my hand and we walked back downstairs. Both Nathan and Caleb were sitting on the sofa.

Caleb smiled grimly. "So, I heard there was a little excitement here earlier?"

I sighed. I didn't really feel like talking about it. I was still embarrassed at my reaction to Ethan. "I guess you could say that. It was really... bizarre."

He nodded and took out a notepad. "Could you tell me in your words what happened?"

I gave him my version but left off the part of knowing who it was that had carried me off.

Caleb gave me a funny look. "So, you didn't get a good look at the person at all? Didn't notice what he was wearing or what he even smelled like?"

Come to think of it, Ethan had smelled and tasted sweet. Almost like candy. Butterscotch or caramel. I decided he must have been sucking on a piece before he'd swooped me up.

I rubbed my arm. "To tell you the truth, I was so scared that I didn't notice much of anything. I do know that he was as fast as the wind. It was scary."

Duncan nodded. "He was quick. He shoved me to the ground, twice, and I didn't see him, either. Just a blur of movement."

Sheriff Caleb put away the notes he was taking and smiled wryly. "You realize how this sounds, don't you?"

Nathan grunted. "Crazy, we know."

"Did Mom show you the video?" I asked him.

"No. She told me about it, though," he replied.

"Let's show it to him," Duncan said.

"Already on it." Nathan grabbed the video from the fireplace mantel. "Someone destroyed all of the other video surveillance equipment. Probably the thing that took Nikki. It apparently missed this one."

The sheriff looked amused. "It?"

"Whatever this thing was, it wasn't human," Nathan replied.

"He's right. Nobody can move that fast," Duncan added. "Or be invisible."

"Maybe it's an alien?" Nathan replied.

Duncan looked at me. "Whatever it is, it's dangerous. And... it's after you."

I shivered.

We all watched the video in silence, and when it was over, even Caleb looked baffled.

Nathan folded his arms across his chest. "See, how can anyone explain that? We've been wracking our brains since this whole thing started."

The sheriff smiled grimly. "Honestly, I'm not even sure what to say about it. It doesn't really make a lot of sense."

Nathan sat back down on the sofa. "What should we do?"

Caleb ran a hand over his face. "Let me take this tape and I'll show some friends who specialize in paranormal research."

Nathan's face lit up. "So you think it might be a poltergeist, too? I mean, that's what I'm guessing it is."

He shrugged. "Even I have to admit; it's *some* kind of strange phenomenon. I just have no experience with this type of thing."

Nathan got up and grabbed the tape for him. "Okay, yeah take it. Let us know what you find out."

"Will do. In the meantime, if you see anything suspicious again, call me. Your mother has my direct number," said Caleb, standing up.

"Sounds good," replied Nathan.

Caleb headed toward the door. "I'll talk to you all soon. Have a good night."

"What about Nikki?" Duncan asked. "How are we supposed to protect her against whatever this thing is?"

Caleb looked at me. "Don't go anywhere alone, keep your doors locked, and don't invite any strangers in."

20

NATHAN AND DUNCAN slept on my bedroom floor that night, just in case the "specter" came back to harass me. When I woke up, it was just after nine the next morning and I was alone. I went down to the kitchen.

"Where's Duncan?" I asked, noticing that he wasn't with my brother.

As usual, Nathan was stuffing his face with food. "He had to work. He's going to pick you up after your shift again tonight. I'll get Mom's keys and drop you off at four."

"Did you guys ever figure out what's wrong with the Mustang?"

He nodded. "It's the battery. I'm picking up a new one today."

I yawned. "Where's Mom? Still sleeping?"

"Yeah, she's been doing a lot of that lately. I think she should quit drinking. She just can't handle it."

"I totally agree. Nice example she's setting for us, too," I said dryly.

"No shit."

Two hours later, she was still sleeping so I decided to check up on her.

"Mom?" I called, knocking softly on her door.

"Yeah," she mumbled. "Come in."

She had the blinds pulled shut so I turned on the light.

"You, okay?" I asked her.

She smiled, lazily. "Yeah, just tired."

I sat down next to her on the bed. "You know, you really need to cool it on the wine. Even the sheriff is going to think you're some kind of lush. You never usually drink like this."

"I didn't drink anything last night. At least, I don't remember," she said with a confused look.

I snorted. "You were trashed. I had to help you to bed last night. You *had* to have been drinking. Even Caleb said you had wine."

She rubbed a hand over her forehead. "I just don't... remember. I guess I must have had some. It would make sense with how I'm feeling today."

I sighed and changed the subject. "So, did his daughter make dinner for you?"

"I... think so," she answered, looking even more confused.

I frowned. *What is wrong with her?* "You don't sound so sure."

She smiled grimly. "To tell you the truth, last night was a bit of a blur."

"I know the feeling," I said, staring toward her bedroom window. Last night almost felt like a dream. I still couldn't explain my reaction to Ethan or the way he'd whisked me through the darkness the way he had. It didn't make a whole lot of sense.

"What do you mean?"

I turned back to her and smiled. "Nothing."

She stood up. "I've got so much to do today. I start work on Monday and have more errands than I have hours to complete them."

"*Ahem*, thanks for asking... my first day went pretty good, by the way."

"I'm sorry, honey," she replied, grabbing a robe from the closet. "I totally forgot. So, your shift at the diner went pretty smooth?"

"Yeah. I'm working again tonight. In fact, Nathan has to use your car to drop me off around four. His Mustang needs a new battery."

She groaned and then nodded reluctantly. "Okay. I'll just have to take care of some things tomorrow, I guess."

I motioned to her neck. "So, how's your skin?"

She touched it and winced. "Still tender."

I got off the bed and walked over to her. "Did you put anything on it?"

"Yeah, I put some Neosporin on it. How does it look?"

I examined her skin and frowned. It looked much worse. "You should really see a doctor."

She waved her hand and shook her head. "No, you know me. I'm just allergic to mosquito bites. It usually takes a while for them to heal."

"Maybe you should buy some Benadryl then?"

"Fine, Nurse Nikki," she said with a wry smile. "I'll pick some up later."

I walked over to the window and opened the blinds. "It's always so dark in here. It's a beautiful day. You could use some vitamin D on that lily-white skin of yours. You're practically glowing."

"Oh, hey... close the blinds," she gasped holding her hand up to shield her face. "The sun hurts my eyes!"

I quickly closed them. "You need to stop partying like a rock star," I replied, amused.

She grabbed her sunglasses from the nightstand and put them on. "Actually, I think I might have an eye infection or something. They've been bothering me the last couple of days."

"Maybe you're allergic to Caleb. Ever since you've been seeing him, you've been acting weird."

She smiled. "It's definitely not him. He is such a wonderful man. I'm so happy we met. It's only been a few hours since we we've been together, but... I have to admit, I miss him already."

It sounded like she really was falling pretty hard for the sheriff. "So, when's the wedding?"

"Oh, God, it's too early for that but I'll be honest, every time he looks at me"—she sighed and her eyes looked wistful—"I just want to jump his bones."

I pretended to gag. "Okay, that's cringey. Please don't say that out loud again."

She laughed. "Oh, just you wait, my dear. You'll meet someone who makes your toes curl and then you'll know exactly what I'm talking about."

I'd already met two guys who made my toes curl, but I wasn't about to share that. "Whatever."

"What about Duncan? Any sparks?"

"Well... I don't know. I mean, we're just friends right now, you know?" I wasn't in the mood to talk about Duncan yet. She'd want details.

She smiled, knowingly. "Friends, huh? Just make sure you use protection if he gets *too* friendly."

My jaw dropped. "Mom!"

"You are still a virgin, right?"

I couldn't believe we're actually having this conversation.

"Oh, my God, *yes!*" I replied, staring at her in horror.

"Although, I know most teenagers don't tell their parents the truth about those kind of things. Just... promise me that you'll be safe."

"Enough! I'm still a virgin and I plan on staying one for a while," I said firmly.

Her eyes softened. "That's what a mother wants to hear. Just know that when things get confusing, or too much, you can always come to me with any questions."

"I'm going to take a shower," I said. "I feel dirty after talking about this with you."

She snorted. "You're such a smartass."

I left her and went back to my room. Instead of taking a shower, however, I lay down on my bed and thought about everything that had happened the night before. It seemed so unbelievable.

Vampires in Shore Lake?

I had no other explanation. Although, I hadn't seen or felt any fangs, Ethan wasn't a regular guy. My own reaction to him proved that he was anything but human. It was both frightening and intriguing at the same time. I knew that was stupid. He was dangerous, although I personally didn't feel threatened by him. Of course, I should. The chemical reaction I had toward him was anything but safe. Even now I could feel myself getting excited just thinking about him.

I closed my eyes and imagined him staring down at me, with those startling blue eyes and that smile of his. After a few minutes, I drifted off to sleep again.

21

"NIKKI, COME TO ME."

I opened my eyes to find that I was in a forest wearing a billowy, white nightgown. I stood up and began moving toward the voice, my feet bare. I glanced down and noticed they were bleeding. Although I couldn't feel it, I was walking over sharp pieces of broken glass.

"Hurry," prodded the voice. It was strong and demanding; it pushed me forward, one foot after another.

"Nikki!" yelled Duncan.

"Duncan?" I whispered, turning around.

"Wait, Nikki!" he cried, running toward me. I watched in amazement as he kept moving without making any progress.

There was a rush of movement on the other side of me and my heart began to race. I knew who it was. He'd come back for me. "Ethan?"

Someone grabbed my shoulders and started digging their sharp nails into my skin. I was shoved roughly to the ground and the shadow jumped on top of me. "Amy?" I whispered in horror.

Amy's eyes were filled with hate. "He's mine," she growled, her slit wrists bleeding onto my white dress. She opened her mouth and her pointy fangs closed in on my neck.

I woke up, my heart pounding. Realizing I'd been dreaming, I sighed in relief.

Someone rapped on my door, startling me.

"Hey, twerp!" hollered Nathan.

I wiped the beads of sweat from my forehead. "Yeah, come in."

"You need to get ready," he said, his hair damp from a shower. "I have to drop you off early at the diner. Mom needs the car as soon as I get back from picking up the battery."

I looked at my alarm clock. It was already after two o'clock. "Okay."

He studied my face. "Are you doing okay?"

I shrugged. "Just a little tired."

"Yeah. We were up pretty late." He pointed at me. "Don't you dare leave the diner after dark unless Duncan is with you."

"I won't."

Nathan stared at me for a few long seconds and turned around to leave. "I'll be outside waiting for you. You have a half hour to get ready."

"Okay, I'll hurry."

I TOOK A quick shower, put my uniform on, and spent a little extra time with my makeup. Then I pinned my hair up and stared into the mirror. I had to admit, I was definitely beginning to look more like my mother every day. I decided it wasn't such a bad thing.

Nathan laid on the horn outside and I rushed out to meet him.

He smirked as I got into Mom's car. "Makeup, huh? Trying to get more tips?"

"For your information, I'm wearing more than usual because I look tired without it. Anyway, I could certainly use the money, so if it brings me more tips, I'll keep doing it."

"I'm pretty tired myself. I'm skipping the makeup, though. At least until I find a lipstick that goes good with my complexion," he joked, checking his reflection in the visor mirror.

I snorted.

He flipped the visor back up. "So, what do you think about last night? Pretty nuts, huh?"

I put my seatbelt on. "It was freaky, that's for sure. I still don't know what happened, exactly."

"I'm starting to think we really do have 'malevolent' ghosts lurking around the cabin. Noticed how I used your word," he said, winking at me.

I smiled.

"I still think it could be the real reason why Mom's renting it so cheap. Maybe Ernie knew about the ghosts but figured it was far better than staying in California."

"You never know."

"I still can't believe that thing shoved Duncan as far as it did. Good thing he wasn't hurt."

"I know."

Nathan turned on the radio and started searching for a song. "It's almost like the entity is jealous."

"Or just trying to get me alone."

"Yeah. Probably both. So, you never saw anything at all? Like a face or a hand or anything?"

I hated lying to my brother but I just couldn't seem to get the words out of my mouth. "Not really."

Fortunately, he dropped the subject.

I'll tell him later, I told myself. For now, it was my secret.

22

WE DROVE THE rest of the way in silence and he dropped me off in front of the diner. As I was getting out, he warned me again to stay put when my shift was over.
"You worry too much. I'm not going anywhere. I'll wait for Duncan."
"Do you have Duncan's number?"
"Shoot. No, I don't." I couldn't believe I'd forgotten to get it from him. Especially now that we were seeing each other.
Nathan gave it to me and I added it to my contact List.
"If there's a problem, call me or him."
"Okay, thanks."
When he finally drove off, I went into the diner and ran into Rosie in the back room.
"How's it going, Nikki?"
I smiled. "Pretty good. We were really swamped yesterday so Susan didn't get a chance to show me too much, unfortunately."
"Yeah, I heard. Since you're early, I'll go over some things with you myself."
"Thanks."
Rosie went over the menus and showed me how to write up meal tickets. Then she gave me some pointers

on how to juggle multiple tables and get them in and out as quickly as possible. When we were finished, my head was spinning, but I felt much more confident about working there.

"Don't worry. It's going to take a while, but you'll get used to it. And, honey, don't be afraid to tell the customers you're new. They'll have more patience and might even tip you better."

I grinned. "Oh, I'm all for that. Thanks."

"You'll do just fine here," she said, patting me on the shoulder. "Just do your best, and eventually things will fall together."

"Thanks, Rosie."

When Susan showed up, I shadowed her for half the evening, and then I was given a couple of my own tables.

"You're doing great," Rosie commented, after I served a large platter of food to one of my tables. "Keep it up."

"Thanks." It was a relief to know the owner thought I was doing well.

The evening flew by quickly. By the time my shift was over, I'd made almost thirty dollars in tips. I was so giddy that I texted Nathan, who was happy for me.

"Listen, is there any way you can work a little later tonight?" Rosie asked, as I was about to punch out. "We could really use you until eleven o'clock. Darlene called in sick and I need all the help I can get. Since it's Friday night, we're going to get slammed again soon."

"Okay. Let me call my ride and let him know. I'm sure it will be fine."

She sighed in relief. "Thanks, hon."

I grabbed my phone and called Duncan.

"Okay," he said, after I explained why they needed my help. "I'll be there promptly at eleven, though I'll expect a tip."

I giggled. "I think I can manage that."

We had a rush of customers around nine o'clock, and I was running ragged, trying to keep my orders right and not piss anyone off. By the time it was ten-thirty, I heaved a sigh of relief as the diner was finally clearing out.

"We usually get another big rush after the bars close," Susan told me. "Just be thankful you're not working those customers. When they're not trying to pick you up, they're puking in the corner. It's really disgusting."

I grimaced. "I bet."

"Funny thing is, they usually tip better," she said with a wry smile. "It's probably because they're drunk and feeling extra generous. But, to me, it isn't really worth it."

Thinking about my mom last night, and practically having to babysit her, I agreed.

"How much did you make in cash tips?"

I pulled out the wad of bills and started counting. Most of them were one dollar bills, but there were plenty of them.

The door jingled and Susan swore.

"What's wrong?" I asked, looking up.

"Customers. Something tells me that things are about to get interesting."

I knew who she was talking about before I looked toward the front door. Ethan. Just like the previous evening, he was with his clan. Our eyes met and he smiled.

Dammit, why is he so damn good-looking?

"Hey," whispered Susan, noticing the exchange. "That's Amy's ex. Have you met him before?"

Ethan's eyes moved over me like a slow caress. I felt my cheeks begin to burn and quickly looked away. "Just for a moment. He was here yesterday. After you left."

"No surprise there."

We watched as the hostess sat the group in my section.

Shit.

"Looks like you get the coffee crew tonight, Nikki," Rosie joked, coming up behind us. "Don't worry, though. They're easy to serve and usually leave a decent tip."

I wanted to protest. To tell them that I couldn't wait on Ethan, but deep down, I was secretly delighted to see him again. Even now I could feel a warm stirring my girly parts. The crazy part was that I knew my reaction wasn't natural. I should have been frightened out of my mind. Not... horny.

"You okay?" asked Rosie, giving me a funny look.

I forced a smile to my face. "Yeah. I'm fine."

"I know... they're a good looking lot. I'm surprised they never bring any girls with them," Rosie said.

"Maybe some of them are gay?" I suggested, although I knew Ethan definitely wasn't.

"Maybe," Rosie replied.

"Ethan used to date Amy," Susan mumbled.

Rosie nodded. "That's right. Well, you'd better go and get things started, Nikki. Maybe you'll get them to order something other than coffee for once."

Trying to appear calm and relaxed, I walked over and forced a smile to my face. "Hello. Can I start anyone out with something to drink?"

Grinning, Ethan stared at me, like a hawk watching its prey. "Coffee for all of us, please, Nikki."

Thankfully, I didn't have to write anything down. My hands were trembling. "And will you want food, or should I take away the menus?"

Ethan held up his. "You can have this one. What I'm craving isn't on it."

His friends chuckled.

I took his menu.

Ethan tilted his head. "Did you sleep well last night?"

"Fine. I slept fine."

"That's good." His eyes twinkled. "After such a crazy night, I'm sure it was hard to fall asleep."

"Yeah. I guess it was."

"What about you? Did you sleep well?"

He looked surprised that I'd asked. "Me? Not really. It's hard for me to sleep when I'm"—he undressed me with his eyes—"hungry."

My nipples hardened.

One of his friends snickered.

"Everything okay here?" interrupted Rosie, coming toward us.

Ethan turned his attention to her and I could suddenly breathe normally again. "Yeah, Rosie. Just being friendly with the new waitress."

She smiled. "Now don't be giving young Nikki here a hard time. It's only her second day."

"Oh, don't worry about Nikki, Rosie. She's in good hands with me."

She chuckled. "That's what I'm afraid of. Nikki, why don't you go pour some coffee for these boys."

"Sure." I looked at Ethan's friends. There were five of them, all different but good-looking. Not as hot as Ethan, but striking just the same. They reminded me of models. The kind you'd see in an *Abercrombie & Fitch* advertisement. "What about you guys? Can I get you something other than coffee?"

One of them was about to answer when Ethan interrupted.

"We're all good," he answered, a glint in his eyes.

I frowned. "Do you always speak for everyone?"

"We discussed it before we arrived." He looked around the table. "Do any of you want more than coffee?"

They all told me "no" with amusement in their eyes.

"Okay, then." I took their menus and then went to grab six mugs. Out of the corner of my eye, I watched as Rosie talked to Ethan while the others sat quietly, listening to the exchange. They never actually joined in on the conversation and it made me wonder if they spoke much English.

Or was it possible that Ethan was like some kind of alpha male vampire? And they weren't allowed to talk unless he allowed them to?

"It's getting late," said Rosie, coming up to the counter. "Why don't you let me finish waiting on these guys and you can take off?"

I nodded, relieved that I could escape to the back room. "Thanks."

"No problem. You've had a long day. Thank you for sticking around."

"You're welcome."

Without another glance toward Ethan's table, I hurried to the breakroom, removed my apron, and grabbed my purse. When I turned around, I was staring into Ethan's eyes.

I gasped, shocked to see him there.

He stepped closer to me. "Leaving so soon?"

"Uh. Yes." I moved backward until I was against the wall. "What... why are you back here?"

"You already know." He touched my face. "I've been searching for so long. I can't believe I've finally found you."

"What do you mean?"

He closed his eyes and inhaled. "Nikki, you smell so sweet. It's... driving me crazy."

Was he going to bite me?

Shit.

"I have to go."

Ethan opened his eyes and it felt as if he was staring deep into my soul.

"What's happening?" I asked, my body responding to him like before. I wanted to feel what it was like being underneath him. His hands on my body. His lips on my skin. "Why do you make me feel this way?"

"Because you're mine. You will always be... mine."

He began kissing me, and just like before, I couldn't resist, nor did I want to. Our lips moved hungrily together and I moaned in pleasure, craving Ethan's touch more than anything in the world. I ran my hands up his back and into his hair, my lust for him as hot as liquid molten.

Ethan suddenly growled in the back of his throat and pulled away. "I need to take care of something," he said, his voice deep.

"Your eyes..." I was unable to look away from them. They were still blue but glowed with an unearthly fire.

"I know. It's why I have to go. I don't want to hurt you."

I flinched.

Looking tortured, he backed away from me, toward the exit. "Leave your balcony door open tonight."

I stared at him, trembling.

With one final look, Ethan opened up the back door and disappeared into the night.

23

"NIKKI," SAID ROSIE, stepping into the breakroom. "Someone named Duncan is waiting for you in the diner."

"Thanks." I stared ahead, my head still spinning from what had just happened.

She looked concerned. "You okay? You look kind of flushed."

I couldn't meet her eyes. I was afraid she'd see how deeply disturbed I was and ask me more questions. "I'm fine."

"Go home and get a good night's sleep," she said. "Working here can take a lot out of you."

I forced a smile to my face. "I will. Thanks."

I followed her back and noticed Ethan's friends had also left the diner. I wanted to ask Susan about it, but Duncan was waiting. I walked over to him, relieved he was there. He was a sight for sore eyes.

He grinned. "Hey. Ready?"

I grabbed his hand. "Very."

He chuckled as I pulled him out of the diner. "What's wrong? Had enough of this place already?"

I released a heavy sigh. "You have no idea."

We both hopped into his truck and he turned on the music.

"You look nice," he said, grabbing my hand.

His smile was boyish, and nothing like Ethan's. There was also a tenderness in his eyes that warmed my heart. I knew part of me was falling hard for Duncan, and yet another part of me screamed out for Ethan.
Ethan is dangerous, I reminded myself. *You need to drive him out of your head.*
"Could you pull over somewhere?" I asked Duncan. "We need to... talk."
"What's wrong?" he asked a few minutes later. We were on the side of a dirt road, not too far from the cabin.
"Actually, nothing is wrong. I just..."
Need to get forget about Ethan.
Duncan waited for me to continue.
I leaned over and pressed my lips against his.
He kissed me back and it quickly escalated. Soon I was back on his lap and taking my pent-up passion out on him. In his arms there was no guilt. I felt safe and protected. So different than with Ethan.
Rocking against his excitement, I grabbed his hand and put it on my breast.
"Nikki," he groaned against my lips.
"Duncan," I whispered breathlessly.
He unbuttoned the top of my uniform and raised my bra. When I felt his hot mouth on my bare skin, it drove me insane. I slid my hands through his hair and moaned as he caressed and kissed me.
Suddenly, Duncan stopped what he was doing.
"Shit," he groaned, staring at his rearview mirror.
A squad car had pulled up behind us, surrounding the truck with its bright flashing lights.
I jumped off him and buttoned my uniform while Duncan tried to compose himself. "Man," he said, looking at me again. "Talk about timing."
"I know, right?" I replied, my cheeks burning.

There was a tap on the window and we both smiled sheepishly at Sheriff Caleb, who was frowning.

"What's going on?" he asked.

Duncan's face looked so guilty it was comical. "Um, we were just talking."

He smirked. "You certainly fogged up the windows pretty good with all that 'talking' you must have been doing. Next time, open one up."

We both smiled.

Caleb went on. "Listen, I'm not stupid. I know your raging hormones probably got the better of you. Next time you feel like making out, though, don't do it on the side of a road. Even a dirt one like this. It's pretty dangerous, especially at night. Now, Duncan, bring Nikki home before her mom gets worried."

"Okay. Thank you, sir."

He looked at me. "Say hello to Anne for me, will you?"

"Will do."

Caleb walked back to his squad car.

Duncan rolled up his window. "Damn, that was a close call."

"Yeah."

We drove to the cabin in an awkward silence. Nathan was waiting on the porch for us when we pulled up, which was good. I wasn't ready to talk about what had just happened. The promiscuous girl, the one who'd been making out with two different guys in the past hour, wasn't me. I tried telling myself that it wasn't my fault. I was a victim. But, was that really the case? I hadn't acted like one. Not around Ethan. Horny, or not, I should have fought him off. I mean, the guy was a freaken vampire, right? He had to be. I was an idiot playing with fire and I was in danger of being charred.

"Hey, guys," Nathan murmured, staring at us in the darkness. He had his BB gun with him and appeared to be holding a tabloid newspaper.

Duncan cleared his throat. "What's up, Nathan?"

He held out the paper. "Read this."

I grabbed it from him and Duncan turned on his phone's flashlight. The headline read: 'Serial Killer Targeting Similar Victims?' There were several pictures of girls, either missing or dead. We both started reading the article.

"They've included a picture of the girl who was found in the lake, as well as Amy. Did you notice the resemblance of the two girls?" Nathan pointed out.

"See, I knew it. Amy didn't kill herself," I replied.

"It's a tabloid. They're not credible," Duncan reminded me.

"Maybe not, but check out the photos of all the girls. It's disturbing," Nathan said.

Duncan looked uneasy. "They look very similar." His eyes met mine. "Some of them even look a little like you."

The hair stood up on the back of my neck.

"I noticed that too. Check out the facial features of those girls. There is a definite resemblance," Nathan said.

I looked at the photos. I could definitely see some familiarity.

Nathan sat down. "What really concerns me are the strange things that have been happening around here. What if it's somehow related?"

I thought about Ethan. I certainly didn't feel threatened by him. At least not violently. "Seriously, I doubt it has anything to do with what's happened to all of those girls. I think the tabloid is reaching for a story."

"She's probably right," said Duncan. "They're always making shit up."

Nathan frowned. "Still, we'd better keep a close eye on her."

"Fine." I yawned. "Listen, I hate to be a party pooper, but I'm exhausted from being on my feet for the last several hours. I'm going to take a bath and then sleep for days."

Duncan grinned. "Do you need any help getting that bath ready?"

Nathan groaned. "Dude, that's my sister you're talking about. Don't say that stuff around me. That's gross."

Duncan laughed.

"Are you planning on going to the barbeque tomorrow night?" I asked him.

He leaned up against the railing. "Only if you're going."

I smiled. "Definitely. "

"How about if Nikki and I meet you there?" interrupted Nathan. "I'll call you tomorrow afternoon."

He nodded. "Sounds good."

Nathan stood up and grabbed his BB gun. "I'll give you guys some privacy. I'm sure my sister wants to shove her tongue down your throat before you leave."

Duncan laughed.

I rolled my eyes. "Nice."

As soon as Nathan was gone, Duncan pulled me into his arms. "So, is this where you shove your tongue down my throat?"

I smiled up at him. "He's such a dork."

"So, you don't want to?" he teased.

"I never said that."

Duncan chuckled and then his mouth found mine. It was a sweet, yet sensual, kiss. After a few seconds, we reluctantly pulled away from each other.

"I know you're tired. I'm going to leave now before your brother comes back out here and kicks my ass."

I laughed. "I doubt he'd ever do that. Anyway, there's always tomorrow."

"Yes. There is. I bet we can lose Nathan by the burger eating contest."

I giggled. "Oh, God. That's right up his alley. He'd win it for sure."

Duncan snorted. "I've seen him eat. My money is definitely on him."

I looked over at his truck. "Thanks for giving me a ride again."

"Of course. Anytime."

I smiled. "I'll see you tomorrow."

"Yeah." He reached into his pocket and pulled out his keys. "I'm looking forward to it."

"Me, too."

We stood there looking at each other. Part of me didn't want him to leave and wished he'd volunteer to stay the night again. His presence was so comforting. I knew he had a lot of work to do in the morning, though.

"Nikki." He grinned. "I'm not leaving until you're safely inside of the house."

His concern made my heart swell. The guy was so sweet. "Okay. Goodnight."

"Goodnight."

I went inside and locked the door. When I turned around, Nathan stepped out of the kitchen with a giant bowl of popcorn.

"Where's Mom?"

"Where else? Sleeping," He sat down on the sofa and grabbed the remote control.

"Aren't you going to bed?"

He grunted. "Hell, no. Someone's has to keep watch. In case any more weird shit happens. Did you lock the door?"

"Yeah."

"Okay. Good."

I felt guilty that he was taking it upon himself to be our watchdog. "Wake me if anything happens."

"I will."

I WENT UPSTAIRS and checked on Mom. I found her sprawled out on the bed, snoring softly. Sighing, I closed the door. I missed her. It seemed like we were always heading in opposite directions.

I went into my bedroom, took my hair down, and then set my cell phone onto the charger. After grabbing a robe, I walked into the bathroom and started the water. As I was unbuttoning my uniform, my phone began to ring. I rushed back into the bedroom and noticed it was Duncan calling.

"I just wanted to say goodnight again," he said, a smile in his voice. "I... um, miss you already."

I laughed. "You'll be seeing me soon enough."

"Believe me, it won't be."

My heart melted. He was the sweetest guy and I told him so.

"You must bring it out in me," he replied. "Because normally, I'm not like this."

"Then I feel really special."

"You are. In fact," he sighed. "I'm just going to come out and say it. I, um, I think I'm in love with you."

His confession left me breathless and smiling.

"I know we just met, and I don't expect you to feel the same way. I just wanted you to know. Kind of weird, huh?" Duncan said.

I lay back on the bed and stared at the ceiling. "No. I, um... actually, I think I'm falling for you, too."

"Really?" He sounded relieved.

He definitely made my heart go pitter-patter. Especially when our eyes met and he smiled at me. I'd never been in love before, but I knew one thing—I felt something very special for him.

"Yeah, really."

"I can't stop thinking about you, and it's driving me crazy."

"Was that before or after I attacked you in the truck?"

He chuckled. "Both."

I smiled again.

"Can I pick you up every night?" he teased. "I figure we'll be at third base soon if this keeps up."

"Oh, my God. Just for that, I'm sending you back to first."

"I'll take what I can get. We don't even have to play the bases; we can just wander the fields."

I giggled and it reminded me of my mother with Caleb. Apparently, I was as pathetic as she was with men.

"I love your laugh. It always puts a smile on my face."

Mine hurt now, I was grinning so much. "You should stop. Before I'm as conceited as my brother."

"You deserve to be."

"I don't know about that."

"You obviously don't even know how gorgeous you are. And smart, of course. I'm not just in love with you because you're hot."

God, he was so sweet. "You're not so ugly yourself."

Duncan laughed. "I guess I'll take that as a compliment."

"It is."

We sat in silence for a few seconds and then I remembered the faucet I'd left running. "You know… it's late and I was just about ready to take a bath." I walked into the bathroom and turned off the water. "I'm going to have to let you go."

He sucked in his breath. "Wait, are you naked yet?"

I snorted. "Goodnight, Duncan,"

"Just give me *something* to fantasize about."

I looked down at the uniform I was still wearing. "Yeah, I'm *totally* naked, except for the nail polish on my toes."

"What color?"

I smiled wickedly. "The same color as my nipples."

He groaned. "You're killing me."

"Goodnight, Duncan. This time… for real."

"Goodnight," he murmured back.

He waited for me to hang up and I smiled again as I ended the call.

I put my phone back in the charger, eyeing the balcony suspiciously.

What if Ethan actually showed up?

There was no way I was going to unlock the door.

His kisses might ignite a raging fire inside of me, but I was frightened to death of him.

I checked the lock on the balcony door to make sure it was secure. Then I went back into the bathroom and finished getting undressed. Seconds later, I had the jet streams going in the tub and my back was getting a much-needed water massage. I closed my eyes and relaxed.

24

"NIKKI."

I JERKED awake to find that the water had cooled considerably.

I'd fallen asleep.

Had someone called my name?

The hair stood up on the back of my neck. I slowly looked toward the window, terrified I'd see something. Fortunately, nobody was there.

Sighing with relief, I let out some of the cold water, replaced it with hot, and finished bathing. Afterward, I got out of the tub, put my robe on, and brushed my teeth. As I stared at myself in the mirror, I wondered if Ethan had a reflection. I decided to bring a mirror with me the next time I worked. In case he showed up. Grinning, I silently applauded my idea. Nathan wasn't the only ace detective in the family.

Still smiling, I headed into the bedroom but stopped dead in my tracks. Ethan was on my balcony, leaning against the railing, and watching me.

Time seemed to stand still as the certainty of what he really was sank in. He couldn't have climbed up to the balcony. Not without a very long ladder, and something told me I wouldn't find one outside. The only way Ethan could be standing there was if he'd flown.

We stared at each other for what seemed like forever and then he pointed to the door.

"No," I whispered, trembling in fear.

He gave me a pouty look. One that looked about as threatening as a little boy. Or, a puppy.

Ethan tapped on the glass softly. "Please?" I heard him say. "Can we talk?"

Thinking about the damage he'd caused the night before with the video cameras, I knew that if he really wanted to get in here, he could. There wasn't much separating us.

The temptation to hear what he had to say was too much. Growling in the back of my throat, I walked over and put my fingers on the lock. I was about to unlatch it, when I hesitated.

Don't let any strangers in at night...

Amy's words.

Sheriff Caleb's, too.

"What's wrong?" Ethan asked, putting his hand on the glass.

I stared at his fingers and remembered how they'd felt on my body. Dangerous, but definitely not in a bad way.

My eyes met his. "What do you want from me?"

"To get to know you."

"Why?"

"You fascinate me."

I sighed.

His eyes bore into mine. "You're frightened. Don't be. I'd never hurt you."

Lost in his blue eyes, I tossed aside the last of my resolve. I unlocked the door and opened it.

"So, does this mean you're inviting me in?" he asked softly.

I could feel my heart hammering in my chest. If I invited him into my bedroom, it certainly wasn't for tea.

He rubbed his hands together. "It's getting pretty cold out here."

I looked down at his shirt. It was a simple, long-sleeved white cotton tee. "Maybe you should have dressed warmer."

He chuckled. "Maybe I should have."

My eyes drifted to his hair. It was blowing slightly in the wind. It looked so soft that I had to fight an impulse to reach up and touch it.

"You'd better be careful. You might catch a cold. It's drafty out here and you're barely wearing anything."

Remembering that I was standing there in nothing but my robe, I cinched the belt tighter.

"So, can I come in? We'll talk and then if you want me to go, I'll leave."

"Fine." I stepped back so he could enter.

His eyes glittered in the darkness. "I need to hear you say it. Just so that we're on the same page."

"Come in, Ethan."

25

ETHAN STEPPED INTO my bedroom and I instinctively put some distance between us.
Noticing, he gave a sardonic grin and shut the door behind him. "Relax."
"Easy for you to say."
Ethan's eyes moved to my robe. "Are you really that frightened of me?"
"I... don't know," I lied. "Anyway, my eyes are up here."
He looked amused.
"What do you want from me? Besides..." My cheeks burned. "You know..."
Ethan's lips curled up. "Your body?"
"At least you're honest," I said dryly.
He chuckled.
"Seriously, though, are you just here to hook up?"
Ethan's face turned serious. "No."
I knew it. He wanted to suck my blood.
"I have an iron deficiency. Just so you know," I lied.
He didn't answer.
"I guess I probably don't drink enough water. I tried giving blood once, and they barely got any, so they sent me home," I rambled. "I mean, I've been trying to hydrate more. Everyone's been hounding me about it. Maybe you could come back another time?"
Ethan laughed. "You're kidding, right?"

I felt myself begin to relax. Maybe I was wrong about everything? He certainly didn't look like a monster. For all I knew he really *had* brought a ladder with him and I was being paranoid for nothing.

He walked over to my bed and sat down. He held out his hand to me. "Come here."

I shoved mine into my pockets. "I'm good where I am. You wanted to talk. So, talk."

Ethan leaned back and stared at me with sexy, bedroom eyes. With him looking at me like that, I couldn't focus on anything else. He was too irresistible. Too gorgeous. Too much of everything. I moved closer, still keeping a safe distance.

Ethan's eyes drifted down to my robe again. He looked like he wanted to tear it off of me.

"Would you stop that?" I said breathlessly.

He grinned. "Stop what?"

I blushed. "You know exactly what I'm talking about."

Ethan sat up. Before I could stop him, he had his hands around my waist and was hugging me against his cheek. "God, I've missed you."

I felt the familiar heat of desire resonate through me. I ran my fingers through his hair. It was as soft as I'd imagined. "You just saw me a couple of hours ago."

"That's not what I meant."

He wasn't making any sense.

Ethan raised his eyes and looked at me. "I know you can't remember. But that's okay. We still belong together."

I laughed harshly. "I think you're confusing me with someone else. I just moved here."

"I'm talking about another lifetime ago."

I frowned. "What... like reincarnation?"

He pulled me down onto his lap and held me tightly. "Something like that."

Realizing he was going to kiss me again, I leaned back. "Wait."

"I already have. Too long." He slid his hand behind my head and brought my face to his.

The scent of candy engulfed me again. I closed my eyes, abandoning all logic and caution.

How could something this pleasurable be wrong?

I mean we were just kissing, right?

Sensing no resistance, he began exploring my mouth. His kisses were hot. Passionate. Hungry. The fear of being interrupted wasn't there, making it even arousing. When his fingers opened up my robe and cupped my breast, I moaned in pleasure.

His lips moved across my neck. "You're so beautiful. So sweet. So... mine."

"Yes," I whispered back, trembling. I wanted to be his. As long as he didn't stop touching me, I would be whatever he wanted.

Ethan's tongue slid down my collarbone to my breast. I closed my eyes as he circled around my nipple, teasing it with his mouth. Soon, I was writhing against him, wound up and aching with a need I couldn't even begin to understand.

Ethan suddenly stopped and tilted my chin so our eyes were locked. "Come with me." His voice was ragged. "I can't make love to you here. It's not safe."

"Yes, it is. Don't stop," I begged, shocked at how eager I was to give myself to him.

He stared at me with frustrated need. "You're a virgin and I'm..."

I stiffened up.

That's right. I *was* a virgin.

My first time was supposed to be with someone I loved. I needed to stop this.

"You're what?" I stood up and pulled my robe shut. "A vampire?"

Ethan got up from the bed and grabbed me by the shoulders. His eyes burned into mine. "Nothing else matters but us, Miranda. That's why I'm here. To bring you home."

"Miranda?"

He sighed. "*Nikki.*"

"I am home. I can't leave my family." I sensed that he meant to take me far away from Shore Lake. I pulled away from him. "You need to leave."

His eyes turned a deeper shade of blue. I stared into them, unable to look away. They were mesmerizing. Beautiful. Hypnotic.

He dragged his thumb across my lower lip. "Come with me. I'll show you the kind of pleasures that most only dream about."

Although it sounded like a cheesy line, my legs turned to jelly as I imagined what that entailed. A burning, aching need began to roll through me and I felt myself drawn to him in ways that I couldn't explain. At that moment, I knew I'd go to Hell and back if he asked.

I swallowed, and nodded, unable to resist. "Okay."

Ethan's smile lit up the room. "That's my girl."

Just then the bedroom door flew open and my brother stood in the doorway, holding a shotgun. "Hands off of her, *pal*. She's not going anywhere with you!"

Ethan growled and moved away from me, his eyes glowing an angry red.

"Did you just *growl* at me? Get the hell out of here, Cujo, before I use this thing!" demanded Nathan. "I'll fucking do it!"

Ethan took a step toward him.

Panicking, I got between them. Somehow, I knew he had the power to rip Nathan apart with little effort. The strength emanating off of him at the moment was frightening.

"Ethan, don't hurt him! He's my brother. Please," I begged.

He looked at me, his eyes still red and glowing. For a second, I knew real fear. He seemed out of control and I didn't know if I was even safe. But then he let out a frustrated growl and raced toward the balcony.

"Who and *what* in the hell was that?" Nathan hollered, dashing after him.

"Ethan," I answered, touching my lips. I hadn't noticed before but they felt bruised and swollen.

Nathan stormed back into my bedroom and ran a hand through his brown hair. "He's gone. I don't know how he did it, but he isn't out there."

"How did you know there was someone in my room?"

"I just came to check on you and then heard you ask if he was a vampire."

I looked away.

"What were you thinking, Nik? That has to be the *thing* trying to fuck with us. He certainly wasn't a normal dude trying to knock off a piece. Which, by the way, isn't at all fair to Duncan!"

A wave of shame spread through me. I did love Duncan, didn't I? I certainly couldn't love Ethan. He wasn't even human. There was no denying that I was putty in his hands. This was much more than a simple crush on a hot guy.

"He did something to me. I can't seem to control myself around him." I shook my head incredulously. "Nathan, God, I seriously think I'd do anything for him if he asked."

He looked startled. "What?"

"He hypnotized me or something. One moment I was fine and the next, we were making out. I did *nothing* to stop it. I even told him I'd run away with him."

He grunted. "So, he *is* a vampire? He certainly wasn't a ghost."

"If he's not a vampire, he's something else inhuman. Look at how he escaped from the balcony. A normal person would have broken their neck."

"To be honest, I didn't see him actually *leap* off of it. One moment he was here, the next moment he was gone."

"Abigail and Amy were right. There *are* vampires in Shore Lake." I thought about Ethan's friends. "And he's not the only one."

"You're shittin' me? One is bloody bad enough," he joked.

I grunted. "Leave it to you to make jokes at a time like this."

"If I don't, I'll go crazy." Nathan leaned forward, to examine my neck. "Did he suck your blood or anything?"

I touched my skin. "He didn't bite me. At least… not that I remember." I ran over to the mirror and checked. "See, it looks normal."

He sighed in relief.

A horrible thought hit me. "Oh, my God. What about Mom? Do you think Abigail was right?"

He swore.

We both flew out of the bedroom and knocked on her door.

"Come in," she called out, sounding tired.

Her room was dark except for a candle burning on the nightstand. It looked like she'd been sleeping.

"Hey," I said, in a low voice. "We're sorry to bother you. We were just wondering if we could check those bites on your neck. To make sure they aren't infected."

She rolled over and gave us an exasperated sigh. "You woke me up in the middle of the night to check my neck?"

Nathan cleared his throat. "Sorry. We saw this news report about some new kind of mosquito that can cause very bad infections. Sometimes even death."

She looked worried. "Really?"

Nathan went on. "Yeah. In fact, if you're not careful, larva could grow in your neck."

She shrieked and sat up. "What?! Eggs! Look and see if anything is growing in my neck!"

We both inspected the bites.

I looked at him. "It's possible, right?"

Nathan's face was so pale, *he* looked like a vampire. He nodded.

Mom's eyes widened. "What's possible?"

I looked again at her neck. The swelling had gone down but the two holes could have definitely been caused by a vampire. Not that either of us were experts, but we'd watched enough horror flicks to know what we saw.

I stepped back. "We have to talk to you. I know this is going to sound crazy but you have to believe us."

Her eyes moved from me to Nathan. She frowned. "I had a feeling there was something more to this than just looking at my neck. Okay, spill it. What's on your minds?"

We started over from when we'd spoken to Amy, her warnings, and how she'd killed herself. Then, I told both of them how I'd met Ethan in the diner and described the events that had happened afterward, leaving out the dirty parts.

Mom looked amused more than anything. "I'm sorry you met up with a crazy local boy, but that doesn't mean he's a vampire. You know what I think?"

This was so frustrating. I knew she wouldn't believe it. "What?" I muttered curtly.

"You watch too many horror flicks. Both of you," she replied.

Nathan growled, frustrated as well. "This isn't fiction, Mom. And I'll tell you something—this Ethan guy looked like he wanted to kill me tonight. Rip my freaken head off. Thank God I found a gun in the cellar."

Now she looked worried. Mom hated firearms.

"A gun? What gun?" she asked angrily.

"Nathan, I doubt the gun would have killed him," I said, ignoring her. "He only left you alone because I told him to."

"Maybe. Maybe not. But, we still need a weapon." He looked at Mom again. "You've got to believe us. This guy is some kind of monster. Whether it's a vampire or demon. I have no idea. But, he flies, he growls—he isn't normal!"

She threw her hands up in the air. "I don't know how to react to this. There are no such things as vampires! Period."

Nathan pointed. "What about your neck?"

"I've never met Ethan, so if you think he bit my neck while I was having a cup of coffee and didn't notice, you are delusional!" she said angrily.

"Do you feel any different at all?" I asked, studying her face. She l*ooked* normal. "Have you had any unusual cravings?"

She glared at me. "For Heaven's sake, Nikki! I'm not going to turn into a damn vampire!"

Nathan and I looked at each other. We knew it was pointless to keep trying to convince her that there were vampires in Shore Lake. Unless she saw it for herself, there was no way she was going to accept it. Nathan had reacted the same way at first too.

She rubbed her temples. "Look, I'm going back to bed and I suggest the both of you do the same thing. In the morning, you'll realize how crazy this sounds."

"If we're still alive," I muttered.

Nathan grunted. "We will be if I have anything to say about it."

"Both of you, drop it," she said sternly. "I'm tired and have had enough."

I sighed.

Nathan looked at me. "We tried."

I nodded.

She pulled the comforter over herself and sighed. "I love you both, but if you wake me up to talk about vampires again, I'm getting rid of cable, Netflix, and Hulu."

26

NATHAN PACED BACK and forth in the kitchen. We were both too shook up to sleep. "Okay, I'm not leaving you alone anymore."

"Fine," I said, taking a sip of coffee.

He wagged his finger. "We should talk to her in the morning and see if she's willing to move back home, too."

I frowned. "But what about Duncan and our new jobs?"

"What about… there's a vampire after you, Nikki? Or should we call you *'Miranda'*?"

I gave him a dirty look. "Not funny. Anyway, what if he follows us? Ethan said he's been looking for me. He had this crazy notion that we are supposed to be together."

Nathan snickered. "How romantic. If you ask me, I think he just wants to get into your pants."

"He almost did," I mumbled, trying not to think about it.

"Good thing I heard those groans and whimpers coming from your room. Which was disgusting, by the way. Do you know how disturbing it is to hear your sister getting it on with a vampire?" he scoffed. "It's sick."

I chuckled, imagining the look on his face. "Thank you for being a worried and nosy, brother. You probably saved my life. At least, my virginity."

"You're still a virgin? Wait, don't tell me. I don't want to think about you getting it on. It's bad enough knowing that Mom's doing the deed with the town sheriff. I'll never look at another pair of handcuffs the same."

I smiled.

He sat down by the counter and tapped his fingers on the granite. "I just don't know what else to do. Mom refuses to believe us. The sheriff will laugh in our faces if we tell him what's going on."

I agreed.

Nathan sat up straighter. "I wonder if we should see if Abigail is still in town. She might have some ideas. She's the only other person who'd believe us."

I nodded. "We should go and pay her a visit in the morning."

He looked at his watch. "The sun will be up soon. I'm going to grab my sleeping bag and camp out in your room for the next few nights. Hopefully, our horny vampire gives up and decides to chase after someone else."

I thought about the tabloid he'd been reading and felt sick to my stomach. "What if he killed all of those girls in the paper? You said they were all similar looking. Maybe he was looking for me?"

He grunted. "What if that *is* the case and he realizes that you are *not* the real Miranda either. And kills you like the others?"

I shuddered. "Don't say that."

He yawned. "Hey, I'm just trying to keep everything in perspective. I mean, we shouldn't rule anything out."

"I guess not."

We headed out of the kitchen and back upstairs.

Ten minutes later, Nathan was snoring on the floor but I was still awake. I stared at the door to my balcony, which was now closed and locked. As much as I agreed that Ethan was dangerous, the attraction I had for him was still there, even when he wasn't around. I wondered if I'd have the strength to say no if given the chance to surrender to him again. It was a terrifying thought.

"WAKE UP, PRINCESS of Darkness," teased Nathan the next morning. I found him staring down at me while chomping down on a banana. He looked wide awake and refreshed, his hair still damp from a shower.

"Very funny," I mumbled. I looked at my alarm clock to find it was already after eleven a.m.

"I talked to Duncan. We're supposed to meet him at the marina around four o'clock."

I yawned. "Did you tell him about last night?"

"I told him some things but left out the part where you were trying to gobble that vampire's knob."

I didn't know whether to laugh or belt Nathan. He wasn't too far from the truth, though. "Thank you for not saying anything about that."

"I'm trying to forget what I saw myself last night. And the unholy noises coming from your bedroom." He grimaced.

"Hey, he put a spell on me. I wasn't myself."

His lips curled up. "I guess you're right. I'm usually the one fighting off the opposite sex."

I got out of bed. "I'm taking a shower now. Thank goodness you don't have to follow me everywhere during the day. Vampires don't like the daylight."

"That's not what Abigail said," he reminded me.

"I've only run into Ethan at night. In fact, he usually hangs out at the diner after dark."

His eyes narrowed. "What in the hell does he order? Steak Tartare? Bloody Marys? Blah," he said, sounding like the Count from *Hotel Transylvania*. "Could you hold the booze and add some of Waitress Susie over there? Oh, she's O-negative? Even better, I'll take two... two shots of Waitress Susie. Blah."

I snorted. "He only orders coffee; he and his five friends."

"Do they actually drink the stuff?"

"I guess so. As far as I could tell, they just sip it and stare at customers."

"Probably planning their next victim."

"I wouldn't doubt it. I'll meet you downstairs in a little while. Is Mom awake?"

His face became serious. "No. This is really worrying me, Nikki. She's not acting like herself. I don't care what she says about the bites being from bugs. Something is wrong."

"I know. We'd better keep an eye on her. I've been thinking. We should probably try and give the sheriff a heads-up."

Nathan snorted. "Yeah, I can already see that conversation going south."

"We have to at least try."

He agreed.

Nathan left my room and I took a hot shower. When I was done, I slipped on a white sundress and a pair of sandals. Afterward, I dried my hair and added a little makeup.

"You getting dolled up for Duncan or trying to reel in a vampire?" ribbed my brother when I stepped into the kitchen.

I scowled. "That's not funny."

Mom walked into the kitchen and smiled. "Wow, you look very fresh and lovely this morning."

"Thanks. I haven't worn this shirt in a while," Nathan joked, looking down at the yellow polo he wore.

Mom laughed. "You look nice, too. Your tan is really coming around."

"Yeah, well, working at the boat shop will do it. I'm outside most of the day."

She removed her sunglasses and looked at the clock. Her face fell. "Oh."

I frowned. "Your eyes still bothering you?"

She nodded. "I have an eye appointment today. I was lucky to get one on a Saturday."

"I thought the entire town would be shut down today," Nathan said.

She looked confused. "What do you mean?"

"The town barbeque thingy," I said. "Remember? We're meeting Duncan there later this afternoon. Want to join us? It should be a lot of fun."

"Yeah, actually, I do." Her eyes lit up. "Maybe I'll see Caleb there."

"He's probably heading up the security," Nathan replied.

"I'm sure. I'll probably just meet you both there after my eye appointment. Keep your cell phones on so I can find you."

"We will," he replied.

She turned on the coffeemaker.

"Anyone want eggs?" asked Nathan, opening the refrigerator. "I don't know about you two, but I'm craving a late breakfast."

"No, that's okay." She picked out a small gourmet coffee cup from the carousel on the counter. "I'm hungry, but nothing sounds good. I think I'm just going to grab a bite in town before my exam."

Nathan and I looked at each other, both of us obviously wondering what she was actually craving.

"Nikki, are you hungry?" asked Mom. "I can make you something."

I shrugged. "I don't know. Maybe just some toast?"

She grabbed the bread from the pantry. "Okay."

After making me the toast, she left with her coffee. Meanwhile, Nathan made himself a monster omelet, using a half dozen eggs. When we were both finished eating, we decided to take a drive over to Abigail's.

"I think this is her place," he said as we drove up the dirt road to the next cabin over. It was older and much smaller than the one we were staying at, but very cute and inviting. Flowers and colorful shrubs surrounded the home and there was a small garden on the side with a birdbath.

"There's her truck." I pointed next to the cabin. "Obviously she didn't skip town just yet. Lucky for us."

We got out and walked up to the porch. I could hear a dog barking somewhere inside and smiled. "At least we know she's not living alone."

"I don't blame her. If I were here, I'd have a dozen dogs watching the place," said Nathan, swatting at a mosquito. "Not with Ethan and his band of freaks flying around at night. Hell, maybe we should consider getting one."

"Something tells me a dog isn't going to frighten a vampire," I said. "If anything, we'd be putting the dog's life in danger, too."

"No doubt." He rang the doorbell and we waited. When she didn't answer, we tried again.

I frowned. "Maybe she's fishing on the dock?"

He stared over my head, toward the side of the cabin, and nodded. "Good thinking. Let's go check it out."

We went around to the back and looked out toward the lake, but there was still no sign of anyone.

I bit the side of my lower lip. This didn't feel right. "You know, I'm getting this horrible feeling. Like, something is really wrong."

"Don't get all paranoid, Nik. She's probably taking a walk or over at a friend's nearby."

"Yeah. Let's hope so."

"You know, the only people dying lately are chicks around your age. I think Abigail might be safe. Hell, you might have been the next victim on that list of missing girls, if I hadn't barged in last night."

I remembered how Ethan wanted to whisk me away with him. He was probably right.

We tried the door again. This time, I pounded on it as hard as I could. When nobody answered, we started peeking through the windows. When we got to the kitchen, we saw a Golden Retriever locked inside of a kennel.

"Aw… poor thing," I said, staring through the glass.

The dog saw me and started whimpering and scratching at its kennel.

"I wonder if we should leave or stick around. I don't want to be here all day," Nathan muttered.

"Let's wait around on the porch for a few minutes. If she doesn't show up, we'll head to the marina."

"Okay."

We sat down in the two wooden rockers she had on the porch and stared pensively toward the dirt road. After about fifteen minutes, I glanced back at her empty truck and sighed. "She's pretty old to be walking too far, don't you think? She drove to our place and we're the closest neighbor."

"Maybe someone picked her up?"

"Like a vampire," I mumbled.

He stood up. "Okay. I'm wigging out a little here myself. You know, she's pretty old. What if she had a stroke or heart attack, and is lying inside, unable to move? Even worse, maybe she's dead."

I rose to my feet, too. "God, I hope not. Check the door and see if it's locked."

Nathan reached for the handle, and it opened easily. He stuck his head inside. "Hello? Abigail? It's Nathan from next door."

Nobody answered.

I shoved him forward. "Keep going."

We stepped inside and were immediately hit with a God-awful smell.

I groaned. "Yuck. What is that?"

"Oh, hell, I don't know. Dog shit mixed with cabbage? It's definitely not strawberry rhubarb pie," he muttered, looking green.

The toast and jelly I'd had felt like it was about to make its way back up. I had to fight to keep from gagging.

Nathan put his hand over his nose. "Let's find her bedroom. A lot of old people die in their sleep."

"Do you think she's actually dead?" I whispered, horrified.

"I don't know. Just stay behind me."

We searched the cabin until we found a room that appeared to be her bedroom. On the full-sized bed were two open suitcases and piles of women's clothing, ready to be packed.

I looked at Nathan. "What now?"

"Kitchen."

Hearing our voices, the dog was now barking its head off.

"Poor thing. I wonder how long the dog's been locked up?"

His expression was grave. "From the smell of things, too long. Brace yourself. Something tells me we're about to see something horrible."

I followed him into the kitchen and we both gasped in horror. On the floor, next to the refrigerator, lay Abigail, her neck ripped open and her lifeless eyes staring blindly at the ceiling. We both shrieked and then ran like hell out of the cabin, toward his Mustang.

"We have to call the cops!" I cried, following him.

"I know. Just get into the car." He rushed to the driver's side door. "The person who did this might still be around."

The vampire who did this...

I got in and locked the door. "What about the dog?"

"Shit." He sighed. "The cops can help the dog. I'm not going back inside."

I nodded. There was no way that I'd go back in either.

"Did you see her eyes?" Nathan said grimly.

I shuddered, remembering the glazed look of horror in that frozen stare. The last thing she'd seen before dying caused that. "I'll never forget them."

Nathan pulled his phone out and dialed nine-one-one. After he hung up with the police, he started the engine.

Feeling faint, I opened my window to let some fresh air in. "I guess there's no question that vampires are involved now, is there?"

"Hell no. Let's call Mom when we get back to the cabin. The police told me to stick around, but screw that. They know where to find us."

"Okay."

He peeled away from the cabin, kicking up rocks as we sped out of there.

"I can't believe this shit." Nathan looked shaken to the core. "Maybe Ethan did this after I kicked him out last night? Maybe her death is my fault?"

"Don't you dare blame yourself," I said sharply. "You didn't cause this. If he murdered her, then this is all on him. Not you."

He didn't reply.

Closing my eyes, I tried to block out the image of the carnage in Abigail's cabin. I didn't want to believe Ethan was responsible, but from where we were sitting, he definitely was the prime suspect.

27

A SQUAD CAR stopped by our cabin an hour later. It was the same cop from the other day. He interviewed each of us and then left. Nathan and I had decided not to mention anything about vampires. We knew he'd never believe it and we didn't want him thinking we were crazy. Or suspects.

"That must have been so horrifying," Mom said, sitting down on the sofa with us. She'd returned to the cabin immediately after we'd called.

"Her throat was torn apart," Nathan said grimly. "There was blood everywhere. It was just... crazy."

Mom sighed. "I bet a bear or a mountain lion attacked her. It must have somehow gotten into the cabin. That poor woman."

"And closed the door afterward?" Nathan laughed harshly. "I don't think so. It was a damn vampire."

She groaned. "Good grief. You're not going to start with that business again, are you?"

Frustrated, he looked at me. "What's the point of even talking to her about this? She doesn't believe a word we're saying."

"How can I?" she replied angrily. "You're asking me to believe in something that's not real."

"Mom, you know me. I'm a reasonable guy. I have to see something to believe it. I saw it. I *saw* Ethan jump off of Nikki's balcony."

"Even so... that doesn't mean he's a *vampire*," she scoffed.

"True. You might be on to something. He could be something else entirely. Like a werewolf." Nathan looked at me again. "Did you ever see his fangs?"

Great, first vampires and now werewolves? Was it *possible*? It was a frightening thought. "No. I don't know what he is, but he's definitely not human."

Mom closed her eyes and put a hand on her forehead. "You kids are going to put me into an early grave."

"No. The vampires in this town are going to do that if we don't leave soon," Nathan replied angrily. "I'm telling you, Mom, we've got to get the hell out of Shore Lake."

She stared at him in disbelief. "*Leave*? We just *got* here. I'm sorry, but we're not leaving this town. I feel safe here."

"Even with the bodies piling up?" I asked incredulously.

"There are reasonable explanations for two of the recent deaths. Admittedly, Abigail's is strange," she said. "But, I'm sure they'll find out what happened. Who knows, maybe the dog attacked her before she put it in the kennel, and she bled to death afterward."

Nathan snorted. "Really? A golden retriever? They'd lick you death before ripping your throat out."

"Never assume anything," she said. "For all you know, it could have had rabies."

"There wasn't any blood on the dog," I said. At least as far as I could tell. "And the deputy would have mentioned something about it."

"Exactly," replied Nathan.

She looked down at her watch. "I'm going to be late for my eye appointment if I don't leave. Are you two going to be okay?"

"Yeah," said Nathan. "Unless lover-boy shows up here and decides to start something."

"Who, Duncan?" Mom replied. She looked at me and smiled. "Are you two a thing now?"

Exasperated, Nathan groaned. "I'm talking about Ethan, Mom. Nikki's stalker vampire boyfriend from Hell. Come on. Keep up."

She frowned. "Call the police if he does. Don't take matters into your own hands."

"Yeah, like I'd wait for them to show up." Nathan stood up. "Do we have any wooden stakes around here? I should check the garage. Or try and cut some of my own."

She looked at me. "Is he serious?"

"I hope so."

Mom groaned. "You two. I tell you. I'd better go. Are you both still going to this town barbeque?"

Nathan and I looked at each other.

"We should," I told him. "Duncan's expecting us and I have a sinking suspicion that Ethan will return tonight. I'm afraid he might hurt you if he does."

"Nikki, if you think someone is going to hurt your brother, then you call the police right away!" snapped Mom. "I mean, seriously!"

"The police." Nathan snorted. "Right. We'd be better off calling in someone from the church."

"Maybe we can borrow some holy water," I suggested.

He grinned. "Good thinking."

She looked defeated. "I give up. We'll talk about this later. I'll see you in town. Have your cell phones on you."

After she left, I called Duncan and told him about finding Abigail.

He gasped. "No shit? I wonder if Ethan was responsible for killing her."

"I don't know."

I had to admit that a small part of me hoped he wasn't. I'd seen both sides of him, though. The seductive and the furious. I recalled the monstrous look on his face when Nathan had walked in on us. It made me shudder to think what might have happened to my brother if Ethan had ignored me.

"Even so, if I ever catch that guy anywhere near you, I'm going to bash his head in," said Duncan sternly.

I sighed happily. "That's so sweet."

"He'd better keep his distance. I'm serious. I don't care what he is. You're *my* girl now. He tries anything while I'm around and the asshole will be sorry."

I imagined the scenario and I knew it probably wouldn't go down that way. Still, I knew he was pretty damn brave. I'd seen it the night Ethan kept pushing him away. Duncan hadn't given up.

"Oh, hell, my dad's calling me. Look, I'll see you guys soon. Text me if you have any problems."

"For sure."

"I can't wait to see you." There was a smile in his voice. "I thought about you all night."

I wanted to tell him that I'd done the same, but the truth was, I'd been too busy concentrating on Ethan. "I'm looking forward to seeing you, too," I replied honestly.

"I love you," he said shyly.

"Me, too. I mean, I love you, too," I said, the words feeling alien on my tongue.

After we hung up, Nathan walked out of the kitchen carrying a baggie filled with garlic. "Do you have that cross necklace Dad bought for you a couple of years ago?"

I sighed. "No. I lost it last summer."

"Shit." He sat down. "You know, I never thought I'd meet someone more dangerous than our old man."

"Honestly, we don't know for sure if it was Ethan who killed our neighbor or those girls."

Nathan stared at me in disbelief. "Don't start making excuses for this... thing."

"He has friends. Maybe one of them killed Abigail?"

"Just stop, okay? Ethan is no good for you. If he has killed people, then you have to stay away from that monster or you'll be next."

"I know," I said softly. After the way Ethan had touched me, I wanted to believe he wouldn't do me any harm.

"He must have really done a number on you. One moment, your head is clear and you *know* how dangerous he is. The next, you're talking about him with starry eyes. You have to shake it off, Nikki. He's bad fucking news. Even if he didn't kill the girls, he's been stalking you. He wants to take you away from us. Your family. Don't forget that."

He was right. "I know."

He reached into the baggie and pulled out a clove of garlic. "Good. Now, rub some of this on your wrists."

I snorted. "Yeah, right. I'm not going to walk around smelling like pizza. We're going to be around crowds of people today. It'll probably be hot, too. No way."

He stuffed the baggie into his jean pocket. "Fine then, let's just go."

28

TWENTY MINUTES LATER, we drove into the heart of town and parked at the marina. Duncan was waiting for us in the shop.

"Hey, Duncan," Nathan hollered.

"How's it going?" he replied.

Nathan grunted. "Seriously, dude, I don't even know how to answer that. This had been a damn nightmare."

"I bet." Duncan walked over and put his arms around my waist. "You okay?"

I nodded. "You look nice." Handsome, more like it. Especially in the light blue button-down shirt. It brought out his tan and showed off his muscular arms.

"Thanks. You look gorgeous. As always."

"Thank you."

He released me and took a step back. "That dress." He whistled. "I swear. I'd better watch you like a hawk."

"I'm glad you like it. I wore it for you." I glanced toward Nathan, daring him to say otherwise.

My brother smirked. "You guys want to get a room, or are we ready to roll?"

Duncan chuckled. "Uh oh. Someone getting hangry?"

"Hell yeah," admitted Nathan, walking toward the exit. "I lost my appetite earlier but it's back. If I don't get some grub soon, *I'll* be the one biting people's heads off."

"Then we'd better get you fed." Duncan put his arm around my shoulders and we left the building.

Since the festival was just a block away, we left the car and walked. There were tents and booths set up in the park and along some of the side streets. The smell of mini donuts made my stomach growl.

Nathan grinned. "Wow, they really go all out."

Duncan nodded. "Like I said, it's the biggest event of the year."

"Glad we didn't miss it," he replied.

Duncan winked at me. "I'm glad, too."

I smiled.

Besides the tents, there were carnival rides and prize-winning games set up in a large parking lot. Although it was relatively early, the place was very busy.

"I would have loved living here as a child," I said, watching as a father handed his little girl a huge stuffed unicorn. The look on her face was priceless and I recalled a time when I'd have stared at my father with similar adoration. Those days were long over. "Without the vampires, of course."

Duncan snorted. "Yeah. Exactly."

The smell of succulent barbequed meat, caramel corn, and corndogs drifted through the air as we made our way toward a huge tent.

Nathan stared hungrily at a woman's plate of food as she stepped past us. He groaned. "Damn, that looks yummy. Lead me to the ribs and brisket, Duncan."

A half hour later we were sitting at a picnic table watching Nathan devour his second plate of food and listening to a local band play old time rock-n-roll songs.

Duncan looked around. "Do you see that asshole, Ethan, or any of his friends, anywhere?"

I shook my head. "No. I doubt this is their kind of thing. Besides, they're obviously night people."

"Abigail said they come out during the day, too," reminded Nathan.

"I know." I stared scanning the crowd myself. "I just have this feeling that they prefer the night."

"If they're bloodsuckers, this would be a smorgasbord for them," Nathan said. "Hell, there must be two thousand people here."

Duncan reached over and grabbed a grape from Nathan's plate. "More than that. People from neighboring towns come to this event, too."

Nathan slapped his hand away when he tried to take another one. "Yo. Don't be stealing my grapes. Get your own food."

Duncan chuckled.

Nathan's cell phone began to ring. He licked his fingers and answered the phone. "Mom's on her way," he said after hanging up with her.

"Nikki!" shouted someone.

I looked up and saw Susan standing alone by the tent. I smiled warmly and waved her over.

Nathan perked up. "Who's that?"

"She works at the diner," I explained.

Susan stopped next to our table and I introduced her to Nathan and Duncan.

I smiled up at her. "So, you got the day off, too?"

"Yes, we all did. They closed the diner down for the day because of the festival," she answered.

"Nice," I replied.

Nathan smiled. "Did you eat yet?"

She shook her head. "No. I'm not really hungry."

He moved over, making room next to him. "You can still sit down with us. I don't bite," he said, his lips curling up. "Unless you prefer it that way."

Susan laughed nervously and sat down.

"Ignore him. He has a problem with flirting and there isn't a Flirter's Anonymous group here in town. He's forgotten all of the steps already."

She laughed.

Nathan made a joke and then began teasing her some more. Susan looked totally different out of uniform and reminded me a little of a younger Jennifer Aniston. My brother must have liked what he saw, because he was totally laying on the charm.

"So, do you know this Ethan character?" Nathan asked, after a while.

"Only that Amy claimed he was a vampire," she replied.

Duncan frowned. "Did she say why she thought he was?"

She shrugged. "She said he didn't go out much during the day and could talk her into almost anything."

Nathan looked at me. "So, he *is* more of a night stalker. That's why we haven't seen him around." His gaze shifted to Susan. "Did he ever try hitting on you?"

She shook her head. "No, but I went out with one of his friends a couple of times."

My eyes widened. "You went out with one of the Coffee Club guys?"

"No. A different guy. Drake. He's more of a loner. Kind of like me. Anyway, I haven't seen him in like forever. He kind of just fell off of the face of the earth."

"How did you meet him?" I asked.

"He used to come in at night. Alone. We'd go out after my shift and hang out. Then one night, he just stopped showing up. I tried calling and texting him, but he never got back to me."

Nathan snorted. "He *ghosted you*? What a fool."

She smiled. "Thanks."

"Did you think he was a vampire?" I asked, intrigued.

She shook her head. "No. He *was* kind of intense, and kept weird hours, but of course he wasn't a vampire." She laughed nervously. "I mean, there's no such thing. Right?"

We looked at each other but didn't reply.

"Did you ever go to Drake's house?" Duncan asked.

"We stopped by once, but he made me wait outside. He lived with Ethan and the others. They rent this house on the edge of town."

Holy cow. She knew where they lived.

"You didn't think it was weird that he made you wait outside?" Nathan asked.

She shrugged. "Not really. Besides, Ethan and the others really creep me out. I didn't care about going inside. Drake was different, though. I wish I knew what happened to him."

"Did you ask Ethan about him?" asked Nathan.

She grunted. "Yeah but he didn't say much. Personally, I think he went back home. To Australia. He talked about his family a lot and how he missed them."

"He was Australian?" I asked, surprised.

She nodded and got this dreamy look on her face. "He had this really cool accent."

Duncan leaned forward. "So, you actually know where Ethan lives?"

"Yes. Unless they've moved. I doubt it, though."

"Maybe we should call the sheriff and tell him we think Ethan's responsible for those murders?" Duncan said, looking at Nathan.

Susan's jaw dropped. "You seriously think that *Ethan* is responsible?"

"We don't know for sure," I explained.

Nathan scowled. "As far as I'm concerned, he's responsible for something. Nikki can attest to that."

Duncan looked at me curiously.

"Hey, here comes Mom," said Nathan, standing up. He waved and she walked over.

"So, what did the eye doctor say?" I asked, after we introduced her to Susan. She was still wearing her sunglasses.

Mom shrugged. "He prescribed some eye drops for me. He thinks it might be an eye infection, but doesn't know for sure. If the drops don't work then I'm supposed to come back in five days for more tests."

"Hopefully you won't have to wear your sunglasses to work on Monday," I said.

She smiled. "Now *that* would be awkward, wouldn't it? So," she looked around. "Have you seen Caleb yet?"

I shook my head. "No. Did you call him?"

"I did, but he never answers during the day. He says it's because he's so busy. I just hope it's not something else."

"Like what? Another woman?" Nathan asked.

She smiled, sheepishly. "Yeah, maybe."

"Are you talking about *Sheriff* Caleb?" Susan asked.

Mom nodded.

"I can attest that he's *definitely* not married," she said. "He has a daughter who just graduated, Celeste. His wife died a few years ago."

"That's what he told me, too." Mom smiled sadly. "It hit him pretty hard, I guess. He loved her very much."

"So what's the sheriff's daughter like?" I asked Susan.

Before she could answer, Mom interrupted. "Oh, I forgot to tell you! The redhead we saw on our first day in town... the cute one? *That's* Celeste."

Nathan sat up straighter. "The hot one?"

Mom chuckled. "Yes, Nathan. 'The hot one'."

Nathan turned to Susan. "No offense, Susan. You're really hot, too."

Susan blushed. "None taken."

"Hey, here comes my dad," said Duncan, waving his hand.

Sonny walked over with a plate of food and sat down next to Mom. He smiled. "Hi, I'm Duncan's father... you must be Nikki and Nathan's mother? The name is Sonny and I'm going to apologize right now for making a pig out of myself."

Mom laughed. "I'm Anne. That's quite all right. I'm used to it. Nathan eats round the clock."

Sonny chuckled. "I've watched the kid eat. I know what you mean. Anyway, I have to be back at the marina in fifteen minutes so I have to eat fast."

I watched as Mom and Sonny began talking about some huge Bayliner he was currently fixing.

"How fascinating," she said, watching him finish his plate of food. "I've always wanted a ride on a beautiful yacht."

He wiped his mouth with a napkin. "Come on by the marina sometime and I'll take you out on a couple. I own a fifty-foot carver myself, and haven't had a chance to take it out much this summer. You'd give me a reason to start the engine."

My mom's face lit up. "That sounds wonderful."

"I hate to eat and run, but I'd better get back." Sonny stood up. "It was nice meeting you, Anne. Susan, I'll see you at the diner again, I'm sure."

"See you, Mr. Hamilton," answered Susan.

"I probably won't be home until late," Duncan said, looking up at his father. "If, I come home at all."

Sonny frowned. "That's right. I heard about the crazy stuff happening near your cabin."

Mom sighed. "It's been a nightmare."

"I bet. Duncan insists that he'll pitch a tent at your place and keep watch." Sonny winked at me. "I don't think it's Nathan he's worried about."

I smiled.

"How very noble of you, Duncan," Mom said, smiling at him. "You're like Nikki's knight in shining armor."

"I don't know about that. I'm just worried about her," he replied.

"That's so sweet," Susan said, looking at me. She mouthed the word "keeper" at me.

I chuckled. "I know, right?"

"Hey, I'm sweet, too," Nathan said to Susan. "And gallant. You should have seen me take care of Nikki's intruder last night. He never had a chance."

"Intruder?" repeated Susan, her eyes wide.

Mom sighed. "Apparently, some guy is stalking my daughter."

"Wow. That's crazy," Susan replied.

I nodded. "I'll tell you about it later."

Her eyes were full of questions. "Okay."

"I'd better go. Anyway, call me if you need me," Sonny replied. "That goes for you too, Anne. I'd love to have you and your family out on my boat."

"Thank you. It sounds like fun," she replied.

When Sonny left, Mom smiled. "Your dad seems very nice, Duncan."

"Thanks," he answered.

Studying him, she tilted her head. "And cute, too. I can see where you get your good looks."

Duncan grinned. "Thanks."

It was getting darker, so the ride lights turned on. Nathan stood up. "Anybody interested in going on some rides? Susan?"

"Sure," she answered, looking pleased. "I'd love to."

I looked at Duncan. "What about you?"

He nodded. "Sure. Sounds like fun. Let's go."

"You guys have fun. I'm going to be taking off," Mom said. "Caleb's supposed to be stopping over after work. I don't see him patrolling the festival anyway."

There were a few cops wandering around but I hadn't seen Caleb around, either.

"Okay, bye, Mom," I said. "Be careful."

"I will," she replied.

Nathan winked at her. "Don't stay up too late."

"Same goes for you, *Dad*," she replied dryly.

He chuckled. "Seriously, though. Text me when you get home so I know you're okay."

Mom smiled. "I will. You be careful tonight, too. Stay out of trouble."

"I can't make any promises, but I'll see what I can do," he said, looking amused.

She swatted him playfully and then left.

WE PURCHASED RIDE passes and then spent the next couple of hours laughing and screaming on them. I watched in amusement as Nathan pretended to be frightened on The Octopus. As soon as the ride started, he hugged Susan for comfort and she laughed.

"They seem to be hitting it off," said Duncan as we got on the Ferris wheel by ourselves.

"Yeah."

Duncan's face became serious. "So, are you going to tell me what happened between you and Ethan?"

29

CRAP.

"NOT MUCH."

He frowned. "So, that guy from the diner was actually in your bedroom? The one I'd seen you with the other day?"

I felt so horrible now that we were actually talking about it. "Yes."

"How did he get in?"

In other words, he was asking me if I'd voluntarily let him in.

I swallowed. "He knocked on the door and I opened it."

"Why?"

"I told him to go away. But then he used his powers of persuasion, I guess, and suddenly I was letting him in."

"He didn't use those powers to try anything else, did he?"

I didn't want to lie to him but there was no way I was going to admit to making out with Ethan.

"He was about to kidnap me and that's when Nathan barged in."

Duncan relaxed. "Thank God he got there when he did."

"I know, right? That manipulating thing he does is scary. I was willing to leave. I probably would have."

"That asshole better leave you alone or I'll manipulate his face." He put his arms around me and drew me close. "The idea of him touching you makes me want to drive a stake through his heart. Literally."

"Nathan said he was going to make some tomorrow." I smiled. "He also mentioned something about building a huge wooden cross and nailing it to the balcony door."

Duncan chuckled. "Good idea. I'll help him."

I told him about the garlic and how he'd wanted me to wear it like perfume.

"I'm surprised he doesn't try to get his hands on some holy water."

"Oh, *that* was discussed, too. Knowing him, he'll rig a bucket of it over every doorway."

We both laughed.

My smile fell. "Who knows if anything would work, though? Or, what he really is. I basically asked Ethan if he was a vampire, but he wouldn't admit to it."

"Of course not. He doesn't want to frighten you."

"Too late for that," I said dryly.

"Hey, don't be scared. I'm not going to let him hurt you."

There was so much love in his eyes that my heart did a flip-flop.

Duncan leaned forward and began kissing me. Very soon, all thoughts about Ethan were left behind. Then the ride was ending, and we were forced to pull apart

"You're an excellent kisser," I said, after we got off of the ride. "How many girlfriends have you had?"

"Thanks. You're not so bad yourself. I've been on a few dates," he admitted.

I leaned closer. "What about sex?"

He looked at me in surprise. "Is it important?"

"No, not really." I *was* curious though.

"If it makes you feel better, I've only *been* with one other girl. We went out for a few months, back when I was living with my mom in Minnesota."

"Do you miss her?"

He slipped his fingers through mine. "You're all I care about, Nikki. I've never felt this way about anyone."

I smiled and kissed him.

"What about you?" he asked, when I pulled away.

I blushed. For some reason, I could kiss Duncan easily but talking about this was harder than I thought it would be. "I'm a virgin."

Duncan raised his eyebrows.

"What?" He looked like he didn't believe me.

"You've *never* been with a guy?"

"No." I scowled. "I'm *not* easy. Just because we kissed and everything doesn't mean I'm a slut."

He burst out laughing. "No! I'm sorry. I didn't mean to offend you. You just know how to…"

"To what?"

He leaned closer to my ear. "To get a guy going."

I relaxed. "Well, that's not exactly difficult." I'd gotten him aroused by just sitting on his lap and kissing him.

"I suppose not." He stared ahead with a little smile. "Well, with you being a virgin, I'd better be careful then. You're like a delicate flower that needs to be handled with kid gloves."

I snorted. "Yeah right."

"Okay, maybe I should tell you to be careful with *me*."

"Maybe, you should. Although, something tells me you'd enjoy some rough-housing."

"Oh, yeah. With you, definitely. Hurt me, baby."

We teased each other a little more and then I spotted my brother. "There's Nathan and Susan." I pointed to the ticket booth. They were apparently going on more rides.

Duncan pulled out his wallet. "Should we get more ride tickets?"

"Actually, I have to use the ladies' room first."

He shoved his wallet back into his jeans. "No problem. I'll show you where it is."

Duncan took me to the public restroom, near the lake. After using the bathroom and checking my appearance in the mirror, I stepped back outside.

"Do you want to take a walk along the beach?"

I smiled. "Sure."

He took my hand and we moved toward the lake. The stars were out and the moon was almost full. Pretty romantic, even with the noisy carnival behind us.

"Hold on. I've got sand in my shoe already." I reached down and pulled off my sandal. After shaking it out, I put it back on and looked up at Duncan. He was watching me with a small grin on his face.

"What?"

He pulled me into his arms. "I was just thinking about what it would be like to go skinny dipping with you."

"I've never done that. Have you?"

"No." He looked toward the lake. "The nights are getting colder, anyway. Maybe next summer?"

If we were still in Shore Lake. We were only renting the cabin and with everything that was going on, I didn't think we'd get the chance.

"You know, there's a hot tub at our cabin. Would that count as skinny-dipping?"

"If we were naked?" He grinned wickedly. "Yea, that works for me."

I knew with my brother and Mom around, it wasn't likely to happen. But it was an interesting thought.

"Great, now you've got me all hot and bothered again," Duncan whispered, rubbing my back. "All this talk about nakedness."

"You're the one who brought it up."

"I did, didn't I?" He leaned down and started kissing me.

I started getting into it, but then remembered that it was just the two of us on the beach. It wasn't safe.

I pulled away from Duncan's lips. "The sun is down and we're a little too far from the festival. I don't think we should be out here alone."

"If he shows up here, I'll kick his ass. I don't care what Ethan is, I'm not going to let him ruin this night for us."

I loved his bravado, but it was dangerous. For both of us. I stroked his muscular bicep. "You're strong but we both know that he's not normal. If he were, you'd have no problem beating him in a fight."

He sighed. "Fine. Just one more kiss and we'll head back."

I slid my arms around his neck and we began kissing, again. Then, without warning, Duncan released me and I was shoved backward. Hard.

"What the hell?" I cried, finding myself lying on my back in the sand. When I realized why, I scrambled to my feet.

Ethan stared down at me, looking more amused than anything. "I was thinking the same thing. You're a naughty little vixen, aren't you?"

My eyes turned to Duncan, who was on the ground by Ethan's feet, unconscious.

Panicking, I rushed over and got down on my knees. *Had he killed him?* I touched Duncan's cheek, worried beyond belief. "What in the hell did you do to him?!"

"Don't worry, Miranda. He's just taking a little nap." His eyes hardened. "I *should* have killed him for even touching you."

"Ethan, you have to stop this. I'm *not* Miranda," I snapped.

He grabbed my hand and pulled me away from Duncan. "Yes, you are. I can see it in your eyes, the way you smell, how you taste..." His eyes held mine and I tried to look away, but it was impossible. "Let me help you remember."

"Stop it!" I hollered, shoving him.

Ethan grabbed my wrists and smirked. "You always did like it rough."

Duncan woke up from whatever spell Ethan had placed on him. He got to his feet and came charging.

Noticing, Ethan shoved me behind him.

"Leave her alone, you asshole!" Duncan tried taking a swing at him.

He caught his fist before he could follow through with the punch. He wrapped his other hand around Duncan's throat and began raising him in the air. "She's mine. Why can't you get that through your thick skull?"

"Stop it!" I sobbed. I pounded my fists against Ethan's back and shoulders, which seemed to do absolutely nothing. Frustrated, I changed strategies, this time clawing at the hand holding Duncan's neck.

"Stay out of this," Ethan growled, his eyes glowing red again. He shoved me away, ripping the front part of my dress. He stared at my cleavage, momentarily distracted.

I looked at Duncan and his face was turning purple. I knew he would die if Ethan didn't release him soon.

"Help!" I screamed loudly. "Someone help us!"

Seeing and hearing the commotion, a group of men from the festival began racing toward us.

Noticing, Ethan swore. He dropped Duncan and held out his hand to me. "Let's go. Now."

"Run," pleaded Duncan hoarsely as he tried to stand up. "Go!"

I backed away from Ethan and then took off in the opposite direction. Before I could get very far, I was in his arms and we were flying across the beach.
"No!" I screamed, struggling to get away.
He turned my head and stared into my eyes. "Sleep."

30

I WOKE UP in a cool, dark bedroom. Candles lit up the room and rock music played softly in the background. I couldn't remember how I'd gotten there or what had happened.

Was I in Duncan's bedroom?

I sat up and called out to him.

Someone sighed and I found Ethan watching me from the shadows. My breath hitched in my throat.

He smiled and his eyes dipped to my torn dress, which barely covered my bra. "So, you're finally awake."

As my eyes adjusted to the light, I noticed he was seated cross-legged, in a brown leather chair. He had on a pair of dark slacks and was naked from the waist up. His shoulders were broad, his arms and pecs muscular and defined. I'd have been impressed if I hadn't been so disturbed. "Where am I?"

"My humble abode," he said with a half-smile.

"Is Duncan alive?" I asked, trying to remember.

His eyes turned chilly. "Yes. Of course."

I let out a sigh of relief. I scooted to the edge of the bed and glared at him. "Take me home, Ethan."

His eyes studied me intently, but didn't respond.

I stood up and covered my exposed bra with my arm. "This isn't right. You have to bring me home."

Ethan stood up and walked toward me. I could feel the electricity between us and hated how I was beginning to respond to him sexually again.

His eyes lowered to my bra. It looked like he wanted to rip it off.

"Why are you doing this when you know I don't want to be here?"

He smirked. "Are you sure about that?"

"Yes. Of course." I took a step backward, my eyes drifting to his messy, dark hair. I remembered how soft it was and even now, my fingers itched to touch it again. "This is insane. You can't hold me here like a prisoner."

"Prisoner?" he scoffed. "If you want to leave, you're free to go." He turned and stood sideways, to let me pass.

That was easier than I'd thought.

Holding my breath, I started past him but didn't get too far. He grabbed both my wrists and twisted them behind my back.

"You said I was free to go," I said angrily, our chests touching. I had to admit, part of me was totally turned on.

What in the hell was wrong with me?

I was definitely going to Hell.

"You are. But, we both know that you don't want to."

"I can't when you're holding my wrists like this."

"Fine." He let go and put his hands on my buttocks instead. "Sorry. I'm not myself when I'm with you." His fingers began caressing me.

"Not yourself? What exactly does that mean?" I knew I should push him away, but a pleasurable heat began building in my pelvis.

His lips found my neck. "You drive me crazy. With desire."

Groaning, I closed my eyes, hating myself for allowing Ethan to seduce me, but wanting him so badly, even after everything that had happened. I wanted to blame it on his hypnotic powers, but at that particular moment, I felt totally in control.

"Tell me to stop and I will," he whispered against my skin. "Or let me show you what real ecstasy feels like."

I could feel his words all the way down to my panties. I pushed away the shame and the guilt, and cleared my mind of everything but the pleasure he was providing.

Receiving no resistance, he tore away what was left of my dress and began trailing kisses from my neck, to my shoulder, and then down to the curve of my breast.

"You're so beautiful," he said huskily, unclasping my bra. Then his hands were on my breasts and his tongue was tracing hot, wet circles around my nipples.

"Ethan," I gasped as his lips and hands grew more demanding. I felt like I was going to fall over from the intensity and force of it all. The next thing I knew, he had me on the bed, his tongue mingling with mine, one hand caressing my thigh, the other on my breast.

I wrapped my legs around his hips and slid my fingers into his hair. I was so turned on, I could barely breathe.

Ethan pushed his pelvis against mine and I could feel how much he wanted me. His hips began moving back and forth, dry humping me through his pants.

I pulled his hair and moaned through our kisses.

Growling in the back of his throat, he pulled his mouth away from me, his eyes glowing red. I was both frightened and fascinated by the fire in his eyes.

"I need to..." his breathing was heavy, "remain in control."

I tensed up, suddenly realizing what he must mean. "Don't kill me."

Ethan frowned. "I would never... that's not what I meant."

"Then what?"

"Take my time."

Somehow, I didn't think he was being completely honest.

I looked toward the door. "I should really go."

"No." He titled my chin so I was facing him once more. He smiled. "I'm not done with you yet."

He seemed so normal at that moment. A young, handsome man teasing me.

I searched his eyes; the fire had receded. I relaxed a little. "I have a boyfriend."

"You have me and we have each other."

I was about to protest when his lips sought mine again. He explored my mouth while his hands moved down my breasts, over my stomach, to my thighs. Soon, his hand was on the edge of my panties. My legs trembled as I realized he was about to touch me in a place that nobody else had—ever. I was nervous but trembling with desire.

"Invite me in," he whispered, a smile in his voice.

"Yes..." I moaned, clutching his shoulders tightly.

"Say the words." Ethan ran one of his fingers over the top of the material. "Nikki."

I gasped in pleasure. "Yes. Yes. Come in, Ethan..."

Just as his fingers began to slide under the fabric, the door burst open and he shot up. His face was a mask of rage and frustration. My heart stopped when I saw his fangs for the first time. "What do *you* want?" he growled as I covered myself with a blanket.

Sheriff Caleb stood facing us, his eyes and face both red with anger. "You stupid idiot. Why in the fuck did you bring her here?"

31

THEY'D LOCKED ME in the bedroom, but I could still hear their angry shouts from somewhere in the house. Caleb argued that he had to bring me back home, but Ethan raged that I belonged with him. Now that my head was clear, I desperately wanted to leave and prayed that Ethan would give in and I'd soon be released.
At least Duncan was okay.
I felt shame as I remembered how Ethan had almost killed him. I was a horrible human being. A traitor. I'd almost given myself to the man who'd tried murdering him.
No. Not a man. *A vampire.*
I sighed and closed my eyes. I had to quit blaming myself. It was all mind control, right? My body was reacting to dark forces beyond my control.
Unfortunately, there was only one problem with that theory. Even now, I found myself missing his touch. Lusting after Ethan and he wasn't even in the room.
"I'm such a head case," I muttered, pacing back and forth. If I wasn't careful, I was going to find myself dead and buried... or a replacement for Miranda.

A short time later, there was a soft knock at the door. "Are you decent?" a female voice asked.

"Hold on." I quickly got under the blanket. "Okay."

The door opened. It was the red-head, Caleb's daughter, Celeste. This time she wasn't wearing glasses and her startling green eyes stared at me with interest.

"Here," she said, throwing me a pair of jean shorts and black T-shirt. "I heard you needed this."

I stared at her, wondering if she was a vampire, too.

"Yes." She gave me a sardonic grin. "I am whatever it is you think I am."

My eyes widened. "You can read minds?"

Celeste chuckled. "No, I could tell what you were thinking by the expression on your face."

"Oh. What are they going to do with me?"

She sat down on the bed and crossed one leg over the other. "Probably let you go. Although if Ethan had his way, you'd never leave his side. My father doesn't really trust you, but he likes your mom and isn't willing to hurt her."

"How sensitive of him," I muttered.

She laughed.

"I'm glad you find all of this humorous."

"I know there's nothing funny about this situation. I've been trying to talk some sense into my dad ever since he laid eyes on your mom. But, he's stubborn and when he wants something, he won't let it go."

I sighed. "Wonderful."

Celeste glanced around the room. "This is *so* Ethan. Brooding and gloomy."

"You haven't been in here before?"

"Nobody has. He likes his privacy."

I looked around, really taking everything in for the first time. It was actually very spacious, even larger than mine, with a fireplace and attached bathroom. The furniture was oversized, dark, and rustic. Very masculine. Facing the four-poster bed was a large flat panel TV. On the other side of the room was a pinball machine featuring the rock band, AC/DC. On the wall, above the headboard, hung a large abstract painting of what looked to be a man, or woman, in turmoil. You could almost feel the emotions portrayed through the artist's point of view. I had to admit, the room didn't evoke many happy feels.

"So, what do you really think of Ethan? Do you have the hots for him?"

That wasn't an easy question to answer. One moment I was terrified of him. The next, I wanted to rip his clothes off. I pulled the T-shirt over my head. "Yeah, but he has that power of persuasion. I don't even know if what I'm feeling is real or not."

She looked amused. "You catch on quickly."

I went on. "Yet, I know I'm attracted to him. I think about Ethan when he's not around." Sometimes even when I'm with Duncan.

"Don't be so hard on yourself. It's only natural to feel lust toward him, if that's all it is. Even I can appreciate how sexy the guy is."

I wondered about Celeste and Ethan's relationship. If there was any. The thought of them being together, physically, made me surprisingly jealous.

I got out of bed and slipped the shorts on. "So, are you guys all family?"

"Not in the traditional sense. But, we look out for each other." She changed the subject. "What about Duncan? Caleb said he caught you two making out. He works over at the marina, right?"

I didn't like her talking about him. It made me incredibly anxious. "Why do you want to know?"

"Just curious. Is he your boyfriend?"

"Yes."

"What about Ethan?"

I looked away. "He's just... I hardly know him."

"He certainly think he *knows* you."

"I've noticed," I replied, rolling my eyes.

Celeste smiled. "He told Caleb that you wanted to be with him."

I didn't reply.

She stood up and began circling me. "Being in love with one of us is dangerous. If you decide to stay with Ethan, you can't live a normal life."

"I'm not in love with him. Like I said, I barely know him."

"Interesting. Your cheeks flush when you talk about him."

I changed the subject. "He think's I've been reincarnated from someone named Miranda."

She laughed. "Ah. That's right. It's been awhile since I've heard that name."

"So, I take it she was the love of his life?"

"Apparently," she mused.

"Did you ever meet her?"

"No." She looked me up and down. "I imagine she must have looked a lot like you, though. That's why he's so fixated on you."

I didn't like the way Celeste was looking me over. Or, maybe she was simply scrutinizing her prey. "So, *are* you people vampires, or what?"

She grunted and wrinkled her nose. "I never did like that word."

So, that was a "yes." "Do you drink blood?"

Celeste touched my cheek, making me flinch. She smiled in amusement and stepped back. "We take nourishment wherever we can get it. Some are willing to give us what we want, some don't have much say in the matter."

"Are you willing to kill people if you have to?"

Her lip twitched. "It's survival of the fittest."

Abigail's dead body popped into my head. The gruesome way she'd died. The horrific look in her dead eyes. One of them *must* have murdered her. I asked her about it.

"Wasn't me. I prefer young blood."

"Do you think it was one of your crew?"

"Honestly, I don't know. I'm not their babysitters."

I could tell she was getting irritated and bored. I needed to know what Caleb had in store for my mother, so I pressed on. I asked Celeste if her dad was going to turn my mother into a vampire. If that was even possible.

She took her time answering. "Probably. It's the only way they can have a real relationship without boundaries." Celeste grinned. "Hey, you and I might be sisters soon. Isn't that cool?"

I rolled my eyes inwardly. Yeah. Real cool. "He can't do that."

"Silly girl. My father can do whatever he wants. Anyway, from the look of things, they're already in love. Both of them."

I had a feeling she was right. If only I could talk some sense into my mom. Even now I knew she'd never believe that Caleb was a damn vampire. I needed to find out more information about them. Ammo. "So, is Caleb your real dad?"

She nodded.

"Where you born like this?"

"No. My father became a… vampire first. He then turned me into one to save my life."

I wasn't expecting that answer. "What do you mean?"

"I had Typhoid."

That had to mean she was much older than nineteen or twenty. "When was that?"

"Eighteen ninety-one." She sighed. "It was a horrible time to be human."

I stared at her in shock. "That would make you…"

"Old." She smiled. "And forever young."

The door flew open and Caleb stormed into the bedroom, looking upset. "We're in a bit of a quandary. We have to get you out of here before your brother and Duncan show up. I guess they know about this place from that pesky Susan."

The news was terrifying. The thought of them trying to take on a houseful of vampires made me sick to my stomach. "Are you taking me home then?"

His eyes narrowed. "That all depends on you."

I looked past Caleb, to where Ethan stood with his arms crossed. He looked furious.

"I won't say anything. I promise," I replied.

Caleb snorted. "Right. I'm no fool."

"Nobody would believe me, anyway."

"Which I why I'm going to let you go."

I sighed in relief.

"You make any trouble for us, though, I can't protect you," Caleb warned. "I'm in charge here but these boys have minds of their own." He looked back at Ethan. "Case in point."

Ethan rolled his eyes.

"I won't say, or do, anything as long as you leave my mom alone," I replied.

Caleb frowned. "I can't do that."

I glared at him. "You have to. There is no way in hell I'm going to let you turn her into a vampire."

He stepped closer to me, a pained look on his face. "There are things you don't understand. Your mother... I'd do anything for her."

"As long as it benefits you," I scoffed.

He looked away for a second. "How do I say this?" Caleb sighed. "Your mother has cancer and I'm giving her a second chance."

32

I LAUGHED HARSHLY. "You seriously expect me to believe that?"

"She has terminal breast cancer," he said, his face grim. "Hell, she doesn't even know about it yet."

I felt sick to my stomach.

What if he was right?

"How do you know?" I asked.

"I tasted it."

Imagining him sucking her blood made my stomach churn.

He went on. "If she becomes one of us, she'll survive. If she doesn't, she'll more than likely not live to see another summer."

His words made me dizzy. The thought of her dying broke my heart. "She could try chemo."

Caleb shook his head. "No. It won't work. It would be a waste of time. Plus, it would be a horrible experience for Anne. You don't want that for your mother. I sure in the hell don't."

"Regardless, this wasn't your decision to make. It was hers and hers alone."

"You're right, I didn't give her a choice. She may hate me when she finds out, but at least she'll be alive."

"Do you even consider yourself *alive*?" I asked.

Ethan stepped past Caleb and put his hands on my shoulders. "Nikki, do I look dead to you?" He stared into my eyes. "Did I *feel* dead to you when you were in my arms?"

I slapped his hands away. "You're even worse than Caleb. You've been manipulating me from day one."

He looked hurt. "I only did it once. At the diner. The first day we met."

"I don't believe you," I snapped. "I'm not as naïve as you think I am."

"I haven't made you do anything that you didn't want to do," he argued. He lowered his voice and pulled me aside. "Tell me that you didn't want me as much as I wanted you earlier. I felt it all the way down to your panties."

I slapped him across the face and regretted the move. It probably hurt my hand more than his cheek.

His eyes hardened but he made no move to retaliate.

"None of that matters," I whispered angrily. "You *kidnapped* me."

"Enough," Caleb said. "We don't have time for this. And you are to leave her alone from now on, Ethan. You got that?"

He didn't reply.

One of the guys from the diner stopped in the doorway. He didn't look happy. "Her brother is already here, along with the guy from the marina. Susan, too."

"Fuck," Caleb snapped. "That damn Drake. He shouldn't have ever brought that waitress here."

Celeste grunted. "What do you expect? Ethan's and Drake's brains are below the belt. They've put us all in danger, and for what? A piece of ass."

"I wouldn't go pointing any fingers," Ethan growled, staring at her angrily. "You've made plenty of mistakes in this town."

She gave him a dirty look. "Maybe. But, unlike you, I learn from mine."

"Enough of the bickering. We need to take care of this mess," Caleb said.

"Don't worry. I'll handle it." Celeste gave me a wicked grin. "If I remember correctly, your brother is pretty hot himself."

I clenched my teeth. "Don't you *dare* hurt him."

Caleb gave his daughter a warning look. "Celeste would never harm Nathan or she'd have to answer to me."

"Party pooper," she pouted, before stepping out of the room.

Caleb looked at me and nodded toward the door. "Go ahead, Nikki. You can leave."

I was stunned. Did he just say that I was *free* to leave? "Just like that?"

"Yes. Just remember to keep your mouth shut, and your nose out of our business, or there'll be consequences," Caleb replied.

I looked at Ethan. He still appeared pissed off but made no move to stop me.

"He won't give you any more problems," Caleb promised. He looked at him. "Isn't that right?"

Ethan didn't say anything.

"Quit your sulking," Caleb muttered just as his phone began to ring. "I' better take this." He answered it in the hallway, leaving me alone with Ethan.

Ethan's eyes met mine. He smiled slightly. "See you around."

I glowered at him and then quickly left the bedroom.

33

THEIR HOUSE WAS huge and very well furnished. I wasn't sure why I was so surprised. If they were vampires and could live for centuries, they had time to save for such luxuries. As I climbed down a large, spiral staircase, I noticed my brother and Duncan standing at the front door. It was obvious that they were arguing with Celeste, who stood between us. She had two other vampires by her side. One had short blond hair. The other had brown hair, pulled back into a ponytail.

"Nikki, are you okay?"

"Yes." The relief at seeing them there, alive and well, was almost overwhelming.

"Get out of the way," Duncan warned, trying to step between Celeste and the other two men. "Or someone's going to get hurt."

"You mean *you*?" the blond vampire said in amusement.

"No, he means you, asshole," Nathan snapped.

Celeste chuckled. "Now, now. Everyone relax. Obviously, Nikki is our guest. She came here on her own free will."

"Bullshit she did," Duncan said angrily. "I was there when she was kidnapped by that fucking asshole, Ethan."

Celeste looked amused. "Such language. Do you kiss Nikki with that dirty mouth?"

"Who in the hell are you, anyway?" Duncan asked.

"My name is Celeste."

"That's what I thought. What are you even doing here?" Nathan asked. "Aren't you Caleb's daughter?"

"Yeah. I drove over here with him. To see if I could help. I'm friends with the guys living here."

"You should rethink your friends list," Nathan replied.

She looked amused. "You're Nathan. Anne's son. She's such a sweet woman. My father adores her." Celeste turned to Duncan and changed the subject. "You're Nikki's boyfriend, right?"

"Damn right I am." He looked at me and held out his hand. "Nikki, let's go."

The two vampires wouldn't get out of my way.

"So, it's going to be like that, huh?" Nathan reached into a satchel he was carrying and pulled out a bottle of clear liquid. "Move it or I'll—"

The dark-haired vampire threw his head back and laughed. "What? Spray us with holy water?"

Nathan frowned. "Doesn't it affect you?"

The blond vampire spread his arms out. "Go ahead. Have at it and see."

"Oh, for Heaven's sake. Move out of the way," ordered Caleb, coming in behind me. "Let her pass."

They obeyed.

I brushed past them and threw myself into Duncan's arms. "Thank God," I murmured.

He pulled back slightly and searched my face. "Are you okay?"

"Yeah, I'm fine." He had bruises on his neck from earlier. "How are you?"

"Better now that you're here."

"See, Sheriff? I told you they were holding Nikki here. How do we press charges against Ethan?"

"You don't. She was here on her own free will," Caleb replied. He put his arm around his daughter's shoulders. "Isn't that right, Nikki?"

"No. It's not right. But, I'm not pressing charges." I looked at Nathan. "Let's just get out of here."

"Where is the bastard?" Duncan asked.

"Right here."

Everyone looked up to find Ethan climbing down the steps, a cold smile on his face. "What can I do for you?"

Duncan glared at him. "I want you to leave Nikki alone."

"We're friends. If she wants me to leave her alone"—he looked at me—"then she can tell me herself."

"Friends. Right." Duncan sneered. "It didn't sound like that was the case when we were down by the beach. As I recall, she screamed bloody murder for you to leave her alone."

"I guess I must be hard of hearing." His lip twitched. "Of course, I've heard things come out of her mouth, but they sounded nothing like that."

My cheeks turned bright red.

Duncan looked at me.

"Okay, that's enough arguing. This is how it's going to be: Ethan's going to stay away from Nikki. You three are going to go home. Everyone is going to move on from this. End of story," Caleb said gruffly.

"I agree, let's get out of here," I said.

"Nathan, it was really nice meeting you," Celeste said with a flirtatious smile. "Maybe we could get together and hang out soon?"

"Sorry. I don't like the kind of people you associate with," he replied, an edge to his voice. "Something tells me that you and your old man aren't what you say you are either."

"I agree," Duncan replied. "Sheriff, I heard you lived out in this direction. Where is your place?"

Celeste's eyes turned fiery. "See, Daddy? I told you we needed to do things my way."

"I guess you're right, Celeste," Caleb said, sounding weary. "Can you finish up here? I'll meet you in the car."

"Will do," she replied with a determined look in her eyes. "Boys?"

Before anyone could react, the two vampires grabbed Nathan and Duncan, holding them still. They tried struggling to break free, but they were no match for the immortals.

"Leave them alone!" I screamed, barreling toward the closest vampire.

Ethan grabbed me around the waist and pulled me back. "Relax. She won't hurt them."

"What is she going to do?"

"Make them forget they were here," he replied.

"Way to go. Why don't you just fill her on all of our dirty little secrets," Celeste snapped.

Ethan grunted.

She walked over to Duncan and stared into his eyes until they began to dilate. "You are going to take Nikki home. You're going to remember nothing about tonight, only that you were at the town festival and had a good time."

He stared blankly ahead, in a dream-like state.

"Repeat what I just said," she demanded.

Duncan did what she asked.

"Good." She turned to Nathan and said the same thing. Just like Duncan, he repeated what she told him to.

"See. I told you," Ethan murmured near my ear.

I pulled jerked away from him. This time, he let me go without resistance.

"Your turn," Celeste said, moving toward me with a smirk.

"No," Ethan said sharply. "Leave her alone."

"She'll talk," Celeste replied.

"So what if she does? Nobody will believe her," Ethan replied.

"You don't know that for sure." Celeste started toward me.

Ethan blocked her. "I said no," he growled.

Celeste sighed and backed down. "Fine." She looked at me. "Take these two and go. I'm getting hungry and pretty boys like these are my favorite kinds of snacks."

Startled, I grabbed Nathans and Duncan's hands and pulled them away from the house.

34

FORTUNATELY, NATHAN AND DUNCAN snapped out of the fugue they were in by the time we reached the car.

Nathan, still dazed, looked around in confusion. "What in the hell just happened? How did we get here?"

"Dude, I have no idea. My head is pounding and I feel like someone put me in a chokehold earlier. Where are we?" Duncan replied.

"Somewhere dangerous. We've got to leave. Now," I said, looking back toward the house. Ethan and the two guys were gone, but Celeste was getting into Caleb's squad car, still watching us like a hawk. I turned and looked at my brother. "Are you okay to drive?"

He pulled the keys out of his pocket and rubbed the bridge of his nose. "Yeah, I guess so. Although, I feel like I was just hit by a Mack truck." His eyes took in the large colonial house. "Who lives here?"

"Someone with money, obviously," Duncan replied.

"Ethan and his vampire buddies," I muttered, staring at the impressive, massive structure. It was white with tall pillars and black shutters. The hedges and landscaping appeared to be kept up. I couldn't picture any of them doing yard work and imagined they had gardeners.

"Why is the sheriff here?" Nathan asked, noticing his car pulling away.

"To clean things up," I muttered under my breath.

They both looked at me quizzically.

"None of this is making any sense," Duncan said. "How come we don't remember anything?"

"They put a spell on the both of you. So you'd forget," I explained.

Nathan started the engine. "You'd better fill us in, then."

I told them everything, leaving out the intimate parts.

Duncan let out an irritated sigh. "No wonder my throat feels like shit."

I turned to look at him in the backseat. I couldn't stop picturing Ethan holding him up by the neck. "I'm so sorry that happened to you. It was frightening."

"Don't apologize for that asshole. Anyway, it was my fault, you know. You warned me about walking on the beach. Thank God he didn't hurt *you*."

I looked at the house again. I could almost feel Ethan watching me through one of the windows. "He wouldn't harm me."

"Bullshit. You can't trust that maniac. Look what happened to Abigail," argued Nathan as he pulled away from the house.

"We still don't know if Ethan was responsible." It had been such a gruesome murder. I couldn't imagine him doing such a horrifying thing to an old lady. Or maybe I just didn't want to believe it.

Nathan snorted. "You're kidding, right? After everything you're still having doubts?"

"It could have been any of them," I replied.

"Did you *ask* Ethan about the murders?" Duncan said.

"No."

Duncan crossed his arms over his chest and gave me a funny look. "So, what were you doing all this time?"

"Sleeping. Mostly. Until Celeste and Caleb showed up. I talked to her for a while."

Nathan sighed. "That chick is *hot*. We should have Caleb bring her around sometime."

I snorted. "Oh, hell no. She and Caleb are both vampires."

Nathan slammed on the brakes. "What?"

Before I could reply, Ethan landed on Nathan's hood, the loud thud startling the three of us. He had on a long black leather jacket and sunglasses.

Duncan growled in the back of his throat. "Not him again."

Nathan stared at his hood in horror. "What the hell? He dented my car!"

Ethan jumped to the ground and removed the sunglasses. There was a very determined look on his face.

"This guy is really starting to piss me off," Duncan said. "Let me out."

"No," I replied.

Ethan ripped the side of my door away.

"Shit, no... he did not just do that!" hollered Nathan. He got out of the car and stormed around to confront him. "What is your problem? Haven't you ever heard of a window?"

"Nathan!" I got out and pushed my way in between the two of them. "Just, stay back."

"Stay back," he muttered, walking over to the ditch. He pulled at his hair in frustration. "I mean, seriously?"

"That was uncalled for," I said to Ethan.

"Sorry." He stepped closer to me. "We need to talk."

"I'm pretty sure we already did," I replied.

"No. You talked to Caleb and Celeste. Now it's my turn," he replied.

Duncan climbed out of the backseat, his face red with anger. "You don't need a turn. Leave her alone."

"Mind your own business," Ethan growled, his eyes turning red.

Shit. Here we go again.

"See, you don't seem to be getting this. She *is* my business," Duncan replied, shaking with rage. "She's also my girlfriend, so you need to stay the fuck away."

Nathan raised his fists in the air and began bouncing around, like a boxer. "Seriously, I think we can take him together, bro."

Ethan smiled, revealing his fangs. "Very amusing. I won't hurt you, because Nikki wants it that way. But, if you keep pressing me, shit is going to get real ugly for you two."

Nathan stopped and looked over at Duncan. "Trunk."

Duncan's eyes lit up.

My brother went back around to the driver's side, popped the trunk, and we watched Duncan grab something from inside. When I saw what it was, I groaned.

Two wooden stakes.

He tossed one of them to Nathan.

Ethan snorted and shook his head. "Really?"

"Yeah, *really*. You're messing with the wrong people tonight, Count Assholio. You're not kidnapping my sister again." He smiled coldly. "So, you wanna go? We'll go."

I would have laughed if the situation hadn't been so serious.

Ethan's lip twitched. I could tell he was even amused. "Relax. I'm not here to kidnap her. Just to talk."

"Bullshit," Duncan said with the stake clutched tightly in his hand. "By the way, I'm pretty sure she doesn't have anything more to say to you other than 'fuck off'. Tell him, Nikki."

I sighed. "I'm tired. I just want to go home."

Ethan mumbled something and ran a hand through his hair. "Fine." He turned to me, looking defeated. "I just wanted to let you know that I'm leaving. I'm going to New York."

"Good," replied Duncan, looking relieved. "Then you'd better move quickly—daylight's coming."

"The sun doesn't scare me," he replied.

Nathan looked at his missing door again and shook his head. "The bill for my car will. You'd better leave a forwarding address, chump. Or pay me before you take off."

Ethan took out his wallet and threw several hundred dollar bills at his feet. "There you go, *bro*. Keep the change. I'm sure it's more than enough to fix it."

"This car is a classic, asshole," mumbled Nathan, picking up the bills. "I knew I should have made Nikki use the garlic."

Ethan turned back to me. "I wish you'd talk to me. There are some things I need to get off my chest."

Duncan moved in front of me. "You don't need to do anything but go away."

"This business doesn't concern you," repeated Ethan, glaring at him. "Move aside."

"Why don't you *make* me," Duncan replied, his hands balled up into fists.

Ethan looked past him, at me. "I'm seriously losing my patience with your *boyfriend*."

I knew he wasn't going to go away until I gave in. For once, I wanted it to be on my terms. "Fine." I moved around Duncan. "We'll talk."

"Nikki, what are you doing? You know this is a bad idea," Duncan said angrily.

"I'll be fine."

"Bullshit," said Nathan, walking over to us. "I'm with Duncan. Nikki, you'd be a fool to trust him."

"I would never harm your sister. Besides, if I wanted to, I could easily take her out of here," Ethan replied. "You should know that by now."

I pulled Nathan and Duncan to the side. "Let me talk to him. Ethan probably knows what happened to Abigail and the others. Who knows, maybe Caleb is involved? If so, we need to warn Mom."

Nathan clenched his jaw. "I don't care, Nikki! He might sweep you away for good this time."

"He's right," Duncan said. "He might use that mind control thing on you."

Ethan, who was now leaning against the car, cleared his throat. "If I really wanted to charm her, we'd be in New York already."

"Great. He's got bat ears, too," Nathan muttered. "I bet he's been listening to us since day one."

"Pretty much," Ethan replied with a little smile.

Nathan rolled his eyes.

"I'm doing it," I said, curious as to what Ethan had to say about everything.

"It's a bad idea. I think you're crazy to even consider it," Nathan said.

Duncan crossed his arms. "I agree."

"I have to do this. For Mom's sake. Don't worry, I'll be fine."

They didn't look convinced.

I turned to Ethan. "Okay. Let's talk."

He smiled and walked toward me. The next thing I knew, I was in his arms and he was whisking me away again.

35

"ETHAN!" I SHOUTED as we landed in a field surrounded by trees. I knew we weren't too far from traffic, from the sound of cars passing by in the distance. I turned around to face him. "I never gave you permission to carry me away!"

"Sorry." He smiled apologetically. "I'll bring you back when we're done. I promise. I just really wanted some privacy."

I sighed. "Fine. So, what did you want to talk to me about?"

"Isn't it obvious? I want you to come with me to New York."

I wasn't exactly surprised. "You know I can't."

"In my world, you can do anything you want."

"We both know that I don't belong in your world."

He stepped closer to me. "Yes, you do."

"I'm not Miranda."

He tipped my chin up and stared into my eyes. "I know that. Look, Nikki, I'm drawn to *you*. As far as I'm concerned, nothing else matters."

"Drawn to me?"

For a second I'd almost expected him to pledge his undying love. A part of me was even a little disappointed.

His eyes glittered in the darkness. "Yes. There's this magnetic pull between us, can't you feel it? We were meant to be together."

Honestly, even now I was secretly excited to be alone with him.

Was there really something connecting us?

He grabbed my hand and slid his fingers through mine. His were cool. "Come with me, Nikki. I'll take care of you. I swear I'll keep you safe."

"That's sweet, but—"

He went on. "I've got money and connections in New York. You'll never have to work. I'll pamper the hell out of you. I'll treat you like a princess."

Admittedly, it sounded thrilling. Wonderful even. But I couldn't leave my family. Or Duncan. "You know that I can't. We're from two different worlds. Plus, I'm still in high school. I can't jump into something like this. Even if..." I stopped.

"Even if, what? You loved me? Don't worry. Your body already does," he teased. "The rest will come in time."

I smiled. "Cocky much?"

"Just brutally honest. If you're having any doubts"—he stroked my hand—"I'll be happy to put my money where my mouth is."

As much as I enjoyed having him touch me, I knew I had to stay strong. That meant not letting him get too close. "No. You definitely proved your point more than once."

"So, you've given me your final answer?"

I nodded.

Ethan sighed wearily. "I figured you'd say no. But, I had to at least try."

I stiffened up, wondering if he was going to try and charm me now.

As if reading my mind, Ethan smiled. "Relax, Nikki. I meant it when I said that I wouldn't force you to do anything against your will. I can't return to Shore Lake, though. This will be the last time we see each other."

The news left me sad. I was surprised at my reaction. "Never?"

"Caleb banned me. I'm forbidden to return."

Even after everything, I stared at the incredibly handsome man standing in front of me, and knew I'd miss him. Whether it was real or not, I felt something for Ethan. There was no denying that.

He looked over toward the horizon where the sun was just beginning to rise. "I'd better get you back. If Caleb catches us together, there'll be hell to pay," he grumbled.

"What will he do if he finds you?"

"Kill me."

My eyes widened in shock. "What? You're kidding?"

He smiled grimly. "No. We've butted heads too many times and he's furious with me right now."

"Because of me?"

He shrugged. "It was worth it, though. I couldn't stay away from you. It's just too bad we didn't get much time together. I was really enjoying myself before Caleb walked in on us earlier."

Remembering how hot and bothered he'd gotten me, I knew it was probably for the better. I'd have given him my V-card for certain.

Ethan's cell phone went off. He looked at the screen and frowned. "Great. He's already checking up on me."

I smiled sadly. "Then you'd better get moving."

He put his phone back into his jacket pocket. "Can I get one last kiss? Something to remember you by?"

What could it hurt? "Sure."

He pulled me into his arms and kissed me deeply. It was hungry. Desperate. Mind-blowing. A reminder of what I was giving up. And damn if I wasn't tempted to throw everything away just to be with Ethan. The chemistry between us was feverish. I wasn't even certain that what I'd experienced so far with Duncan was as intense or passionate. As these thoughts ran through my head, I began to notice a chill radiating from him.

I pulled back. "You're freezing. Are you sick?"

Ethan looked embarrassed. "No. It happens when I'm hungry. I used up a lot of my energy today and haven't fed yet. This last flight really did a number on me."

I searched his eyes. "So, you really are... a vampire?"

I could tell he was reluctant to answer, but he eventually nodded.

I stared at his mouth. "I saw the fangs but wasn't totally sure."

"So, the flying and the super-strength didn't give anything away?" he joked.

"Maybe a little."

He smiled sadly.

I studied his face. It seemed unusually pale. I hadn't noticed it before. "So, your diet consists of blood?"

"Do you really want to know?"

I thought of Abigail again. "Yes. I guess I do."

It took him awhile to answer. "I'm not a murderer, Nikki. I feed only from willing participants. I take what I need, but it doesn't kill them."

"Does it hurt?" I asked. "When you take it?"

"It can but it doesn't have to. I try to make the experience very pleasant."

"What happens if you stop drinking blood?"

"I'd wither away and die. Just like you would, without food and water. Although, it happens much more quickly with us."

"So, you can't eat pizza or cheeseburgers or anything like that?"

"No. Just maybe a few nuts and berries. Liquids are okay. They don't really hold any value, though. Blood is the only thing that provides the nutrients we need to survive."

"I see." He was starting to look almost... sickly. "You need it now, don't you?"

Desperately.

He nodded. "Just give me a minute while I summon up the strength to bring you back to the car. Then I'll worry about it afterward."

"I could walk back to the car, so you can save your strength."

"It's too far. Besides, I need to leave for New York, anyway. I'm heading in that direction."

"Where are you going to find a willing participant at this time of night?"

"I'll figure something out." He looked toward the grass. "I just need to find a rabbit or something out here."

I gave him a funny look. "Bugs Bunny?"

"Hey, it's not my first choice either," he replied, smiling in amusement. "Their blood lacks many things. But, it's better than nothing. It will at least keep me going until I can find something more substantial."

"What about me?" I asked, surprising myself.

He frowned. "You?"

I pulled my hair away from my neck. "Yes. It's too dangerous for you to be in this state. Especially with Caleb after you. So, use my blood."

Ethan didn't move. His eyes glowed, however. I knew he was struggling with the temptation.

I touched is arm. "Come on. Do it before I change my mind. You said it won't hurt, right?"

He stared at my neck. "It won't. It'll just leave you a little lightheaded." Ethan sighed. "I don't want you to think I was trying to trick you into this."

"I know. I was the one who brought it up. This isn't going to make me a vampire, is it?"

He shook his head.

"Okay. Then, go for it."

"Your generosity is... overwhelming. I don't know what to say."

"Just make sure you don't kill me."

"Never." He caressed my neck with his fingers. "Nikki, look at me."

Our eyes met. His began to dilate and I soon found myself deeply relaxed. Maybe even pleasantly tipsy.

"You're sure about this?"

I could feel his breath against my skin. It gave me goosebumps. I closed my eyes. "Yes, Ethan."

He licked my neck, causing a tingling sensation.

"Sweet, sweet Nikki. I've never felt this way about anyone. You've taken my heart and have given me much more than what I deserve," he whispered.

Startled at his admission, I opened my eyes just as his teeth penetrated my skin. There was a slight pinch and then an intense rush of blissful pleasure as my blood flowed into Ethan. Aroused, I held him tightly, riding wave after wave of divine pleasure until all at once, I found myself shuddering in ecstasy.

"Wow," I whispered, trembling.

Ethan moved his hand over my breasts. He was warm now, and I could feel his excitement pressing against my stomach. I writhed against him and moaned as his fingers moved between my legs.

A gunshot echoed through the night. He withdrew from my neck, a look of horror and pain etched across his face.

Realizing that someone had shot him, I reached my hand out. "No!" I screamed.

Ethan backed away, and then in a blink of an eye, was gone.

Trembling, I sank to my knees. I was frightened, but too dazed to do anything about it.

"Did you get him?!" hollered my mother's voice in the distance.

"Yeah," Caleb said, his voice getting nearer. "He's bleeding. He won't get far."

"Mom?" I called out.

She crashed through the bushes and was suddenly by my side. "Nikki! Oh, my God, you're bleeding everywhere." She tried helping me up, but I didn't have the strength to stand. "Caleb, hurry! We have to get her to the hospital!"

"I've already called an ambulance," I heard him say.

I lay my head down in the grass. "Mom..." My eyelids grew heavy. I wanted to warn her about Caleb, but I was so tired. So exhausted.

She raised my head to her lap and began stroking my hair. "My poor sweet girl. Are you okay?"

"Yes. Just tired..." I closed my eyes again. I just needed to rest for a little while.

"Don't fall asleep!" she cried. "You have to stay with us. Do you hear me? Oh, my God, Caleb, she's so pale. What was he doing to my little girl?"

Giving in to the darkness, I missed his reply.

End of Book One

Printed in Great Britain
by Amazon